"Colorful characters and a cheerfully compelling tone, all combined to make a mystery worth barking about."
—*Linda O. Johnson, author of* THE MORE THE TERRIER, *Berkley Prime Crime*

Yes, Melinda has been feuding with Mona, the queen of Laguna Beach's dog-loving divas. But Mel never expected Mona to end up murdered.

Mona loved Fluffy. No, Mona worshipped Fluffy. She'd never abandon her dog.

Something was wrong. Why would Mona leave her front door unlocked, the alarm off and her cell phone behind?

Fluffy shoved me out of the way and trotted down the hallway to the next room.

I'd barely turned the knob when Fluffy barged past me, head-butting the door against the wall with a loud bang.

I stumbled through the doorway. It wasn't a room. It was a mini-palace fit for a movie star. Fluffy's palace. A white sheepskin rug in front of her personal fireplace, a king sized sleigh bed and a dressing screen (why a dog needed a dressing screen was beyond me). Fresh filtered water dripped into her Wedgewood doggie bowl.

It was also a disaster.

Fluffy's wardrobe was strewn throughout the room, draped precariously on the bed, and hanging out of open drawers. While Mona had an obscene amount of photos, Fluffy had her own slew of trophies and ribbons. All of them haphazardly tossed about.

The room looked like it had been ransacked.

Fluffy disappeared behind the disheveled bed. Her tail stopped wagging, and she whined softly.

That's when I saw her.

At first, I wasn't certain what I was looking at. Then it became clear. Mona was sprawled on the floor as if posing for a men's magazine. It was almost picture perfect, except for the blood matting her five-hundred-dollar haircut and the gold statue stuck in her head.

I hesitantly moved closer. Fluffy nuzzled Mona's cheek. When she didn't move, Fluffy pawed her shoulder, still whining.

"I don't think she's getting up, girl," I said softly.

Mona was deader than a stuffed Poodle.

Get Fluffy

by

Sparkle Abbey

Bell Bridge Books

Bell Bridge Books
PO BOX 300921
Memphis, TN 38130
Print ISBN: 978-1-61194-121-0

Bell Bridge Books is an Imprint of BelleBooks, Inc.

Printed and bound in the United States of America.

We at BelleBooks enjoy hearing from readers.
Visit our websites – www.BelleBooks.com and www.BellBridgeBooks.com.

10 9 8 7 6 5 4 3 2 1

Cover design: Debra Dixon
Interior design: Hank Smith
Photo credits:
Woman/Dog illustration - © Fanny71 | Dreamstime.com
Collar © Roughcollie | Dreamstime.com
Paw Print - © Booka1 | Dreamstime.com
Magnifying glass - © Yudesign | Dreamstime.com

:Lfg:01:

Dedication

This book is dedicated to Team Sparkle Abbey. An amazing group of friends and family, who enthusiastically attend book signings, handout bookmarks, master our website and ask perfect strangers what they're reading. Thank-you will never be enough.

Chapter One

I am nothing like my cousin, Caro, the "pet shrink."

She's a redhead, I'm a brunette. She's kept her Texas twang, I busted my butt to lose mine. (Except when I'm honked off, then my southern drawl can strike like a Gulf coast hurricane.) She's calm and direct. I'm equally direct. As for calm, I have to admit, sometimes my emotions tend to overrule my better judgment.

So who would have thought I'd end up in the middle of a Laguna Beach murder investigation, just like Caro?

From my very first breath, Mama had groomed me to be Miss America, just like her and her sister, Katherine. Or a Dallas Cowboy Cheerleader, which in Texas was the more prestigious of the two. By my twenty-first birthday, I'd gathered ten first-place pageant crowns like Fourth of July parade candy. That's when my beauty queen career had been dethroned in public scandal.

Everyone believed she "encouraged" a male judge to cast his vote for me. As for what I thought, well, no daughter wants to believe her mama is a hustler. To this day, Mama still won't talk about *The Incident* above a whisper.

With the battle for the top crown over, I'd traded in my tiaras, sashes and hair spray for Swarovski crystal collars, cashmere dog sweaters and botanical flea dip. I left Texas and moved to Laguna Beach, California, a community known for its art, wealth and love of dogs. I opened Bow Wow Boutique and catered to the canine who had everything.

I loved Laguna. Loved running my own business. I even loved the quirky folks whose lives revolved around their pooches. But sometimes I longed for Texas—wide open spaces, cowboy boots and big-big hair. Who wouldn't?

It was mid-October. The tourists had packed up and headed home. The locals ventured out of their gated communities to enjoy all the beachside town had to offer. Most importantly, there was available parking downtown. At least until next May.

The annual Fur Ball had finally arrived—a community event to raise money for the Laguna Beach Animal Rescue League. The balmy weather was perfect for an outdoor fundraiser.

As always at these shindigs, the humans coughed up large chunks of dough for a worthy cause. Breezy air kisses and alcohol flowed freely, while we all pretended to be best friends. Trust me, we were one society catfight away from a hell of an entertaining evening.

I looked down at Missy, my English Bulldog, who waited patiently at my feet. Her crystal-studded tiara sat lopsided on the top of her head, and a small puddle of drool had collected between her paws.

I straightened her crown and whispered, "We're up, girl. Let's show them what we've got."

With our heads held high, Missy and I strutted our stuff down the red carpet. The pup-a-razzi cameras flashed, and the crowd cheered. One reporter asked who'd made my strapless leather gown (Michael Kors) and another wanted to know how Missy had won her tiara (she'd placed first in Laguna Beach's Ugliest Bulldog contest last year).

Once we reached the end of the walkway, I leaned down to dab the drool from Missy's chin. "You did great." I kissed the top of her head. "Let's go find our friends."

Missy gave my hand a slobbery kiss, and then we made our way into the main event. Under an extravagant white tent and glittering lights, two hundred wealthy dog lovers and their four-legged friends paraded around in designer rags, both human and canine dripped with diamonds.

I quickly spotted Kimber Shores and her pug Noodles making their way in our direction. Kimber oozed understated glamour in her mauve jumpsuit. She'd definitely make Laguna's Best-Dressed List.

"Mel, I'm so glad I found you," she declared.

As we air kissed, the low-cut back of her outfit offered a glimpse of her many tattoos.

"Noodles looks amazing," she continued in her melodious voice. "I'm so glad you talked me out of the velvet jacket."

Kimber and her pug had stopped by the shop earlier. Noodles had been in desperate need of a wardrobe update. I'd managed to wrangle him out of his Hugh Hefner smoking jacket and into a modest white tux and tails. Noodles sat in front of Missy, his marble eyes watching the slobber slide down the corners of her mouth.

I smiled affectionately. "He really isn't a velvet kinda guy. I love the top hat. Nice choice."

Out of the corner of my eye I could see Grey Donovan, my fiancé of two years, heading in our direction. Kimber must have noticed, too; she immediately looked uncomfortable.

To the outside world, Grey's and my relationship was seen as a tad unorthodox. We were the on-again, off-again type. Presently, we were "on."

"Ah, I see you're not alone. Anyway, I just wanted to say thanks." She grabbed my hand and squeezed.

"You're welcome. Stop by Bow Wow when you get a chance. I have the perfect sweater-vest for Noodles."

Kimber and her pug disappeared into the crowd just as Grey arrived.

"Caro and Diana organized a great event." He handed me a glass of pinot noir. He looked amazing in his black tux. But then, he always looked good.

Missy sniffed his pant leg, double-checking he hadn't stepped out on her. He bent down and gave her some love. She snorted happily, lapping up Grey's affection. I knew exactly how she felt.

I took a sip of wine, appreciating the black-pepper finish. I snagged us each a tomato and goat cheese tart from a passing waiter (he was out of pigs-in-a-blanket, Missy's favorite).

"I hate to break it to you, but it's the Dallas upbringing. Every society girl knows how to throw a successful charity fundraiser by her eighteenth birthday." I took a bite of the tart and sighed. Delicious. "But you're right. It's a fabulous evening."

Grey, an undercover FBI agent, worked white-collar crime—mostly art theft. He could be gone for two days or two months without a whisper of his well-being. I never knew if he was sipping espresso in Paris or being held hostage in a deserted warehouse in East LA.

His decision to keep me completely in the dark of his activities—his way of protecting me—had finally pushed me to the breaking point. I'd realized if I had trouble *dating* Grey, our marriage could end up a disaster. So I'd called off the wedding (two months before the big day), causing a swirl of rumors and speculation.

I swear, I'd tried to return the six-carat sapphire engagement ring that had belonged to his great-grandmother, but Grey had refused to accept it. He believed we could work it out. I really wanted him to be right.

"To Caro and Diana. May the evening continue to be a howling success." Grey lifted his glass, and I followed suit.

We mingled with the other guests and made our way to the table of auction items. I spotted my cousin next to the open bar, schmoozing with a celebrity dog trainer who currently judged a TV reality pet show. I didn't have to hear her southern drawl to know she'd used it to her advantage.

She fooled a lot of people at first glance. She looked as soft as a hothouse wildflower, but inside she was all iron and grit.

At the moment, Caro and I weren't exactly speaking. Since our childhood, Caro had always saved something or someone. A few years ago that had included her ex-husband who deserved to rot behind prison walls instead.

To this day, she continued to analyze how her marriage had fallen apart. I'd expressed my opinion (truth be told, it was unsolicited at the time, but that hadn't stopped me), and Caro got her feelings hurt. We had *words.*

I know I'm the one who should apologize first but, knowing me, my smartass mouth would probably make matters worse. Sometimes I'm better with dogs than people.

Recently, I'd broken my vow of silence. Caro's best friend, Diana Knight, a former movie star and one of Laguna's resident celebrities, had been arrested for murder. In my experience, who better to deliver bad news than family?

Luckily for Diana, she was one of Caro's success stories. Caro had helped clear Diana of a bogus murder wrap and in the process had almost gotten herself killed. Thankfully, the police—and her quick thinking—had saved her.

A slow smile tugged the corners of my mouth as I waited for my cousin to turn in my direction.

Competition runs deep in the Montgomery blood, our mothers' side of the family tree. Over the years, Caro had managed to intermittently suppress her competitiveness. I, on the other hand, let mine run free. Electrified with the sudden possibility of getting the best of my cousin, I grabbed Grey's arm. "Let's go say hi to Caro."

"No." He didn't even take his eye off the list of silent auction items.

"Come on. You just said she did a great job."

"I'm not going to be a vehicle for you to flaunt that thing." He flicked his auction list toward the gaudy, but sentimental, brooch pinned strategically to my gown.

The pin was a family heirloom, a twenty-two karat gold basket filled with fruit made of precious gems. Rubies, diamonds, emeralds and topaz. You'd never know by looking at the garish thing that it was insured for more money than all four years of my Stanford college tuition.

I adjusted the brooch. "It gives my little black dress something extra."

Grey's green eyes softened. His gaze traveled from the bottom of my floor length, strapless, leather gown and ended at the gaudy heirloom.

I felt the heat flood my checks and pretended his blatant appraisal didn't make my knees weak.

"*Little* is one description. Leave your cousin alone," he said on a sigh.

Poor Grey. He was my fiancé, but he was also Caro's friend.

"Grandma Tillie left the pin to me. I only retrieved what was rightfully mine." Grandma was very specific in her will. The brooch was to go to her "*favorite* granddaughter." That was me. Then again, Caro was just as convinced it was her.

"You broke into Caro's house and stole it," he said.

"Only after she'd marched into Bow Wow Boutique, in the middle of the day, and stole it from my purse in front of God and my customers."

He looked at me as if I'd lost my mind. "So that makes breaking into her private safe okay?"

I grimaced. There was a tingle of regret about my actions that day. It had taken a few tries to figure out the combination, but I had.

Caro hadn't used an easy-to-hack combination. No. She'd used something much more personal that only I could truly understand the significance of.

When I thought about that, I felt like a traitor who deserved to be shot at twenty paces. So, I tried not to think about it.

I was sure I'd pay for my transgression at some point.

"Mel, do you want the brooch, or to make Carolina squirm?" Grey asked.

"Is there a right or wrong answer?"

"Yes."

I took another sip of wine, letting the warmth from the alcohol seep through me. I know it's selfish, but I wanted both. Hey, at least I'm honest.

Caro finally turned and caught my eye. I held back the urge to jump up and down. Instead, I lifted my wine glass in salute, making sure she could see I had on the brooch.

She hesitated for a second, aware we were gossip prey. Like the southern lady she was, she returned the salute with an amused smile. We both knew she was plotting revenge. *Game on, cousin.* I'd have to find a better hiding place than my cookie jar.

Grey shook his head in defeat and directed my attention to the banquet tables of donated items for the silent auction. There was one item that had me seriously contemplating going home for my credit card. An African safari. I sighed, knowing I was about to spend too much money, and I wasn't even buzzed.

"You're doing the right thing," Grey said.

"I've always wanted to go on an African safari."

"I was talking about Caro."

"I do have some self-control." I set my glass on the table and adjusted his bow tie. Not because it needed it. But because it was our first public appearance since the almost-wedding.

"I just wanted her to see I had it," I explained.

"I don't always understand you two. Or why your friends encourage your harebrained competition."

I retrieved my glass with a shrug. "Because it's harmless fun."

I scribbled an obscene dollar amount alongside my bidding number on the safari listing, knowing I'd bumped the mayor out of the playing field.

Grey whistled softly. "Playing to win?"

"Why else would I play?"

"If I could have your attention," Amelia Hudges, the ARL director, spoke into the microphone.

Everyone turned expectantly in Amelia's direction. I almost choked on my wine. Amelia looked like an over-the-top Bette Midler with her frizzed-out orange hair and heavily beaded gown. *Good God.* Had someone died and covered the mirrors in her house?

"We've made some quick calculations after a few passes around the room." She paced the stage in excitement. "Due to your generosity, the silent auction has already grossed an estimated two hundred fifty thousand dollars." Amelia's high-pitched twitter competed with resounding applause and excited barking.

"Now it's time to get serious." She raised a freckled hand for silence. "We're more than halfway to our goal of three hundred fifty thousand dollars. Listen to your heart, not your accountant. Open your wallets, and let's start the live auction! Find your seats, everyone."

Grey, Missy and I ping-ponged through the noisy crowd and were the last of our group to arrive. We were about to sit when Tova Randall, a highly successful lingerie model who had just moved to town, called out my name.

Everyone at our table watched as Tova bounced closer. It wasn't her perfect pale complexion or her luxurious auburn hair that drew our attention. It was her blush-pink, silk-taffeta gown hugging her famous curves. Those same curves had paid for her thirteen million dollar home in the hills, down the street from Grey's place.

"Melinda Langston, you owe me fifteen hundred dollars," she announced in a not-so-conversational tone.

"I beg your pardon?"

She was drunk. It was the only plausible explanation. I looked at our tablemates and shook my head apologetically.

Unlike Tova, her Yorkiepoo loved me. And I loved Kiki in return. Her pink, mini-taffeta dress rustled as her tiny five-pound body wiggled in excitement. I reached down to pet the adorable dog. Kiki immediately rewarded me with enthusiastic kisses.

Missy sniffed Tova's pocket puppy in the universal dog greeting. Unimpressed, Missy crawled under the table, looking for a spot to nap.

Tova gripped the diamond encrusted leash tighter, pulling Kiki closer to her. "You gave my baby fleas," she huffed.

Hells bells. What was she talking about?

Chapter Two

A loud murmur rippled over our table. All eyes were on us, waiting for my reaction to Tova's outrageous claim.

I set my half-empty glass of pinot noir next to my plate. "I don't know what you're talking about."

Tova lifted her chin higher. "Kiki and I got kicked out of *Mommy and Doggie Yoga* because she had fleas."

Seriously, how was that my fault? Besides, it wasn't the end of the world. It happens to the best of dogs (although Missy's never been afflicted with them). I'm sure even Rin Tin Tin had a case of fleas. Once.

"That must have been embarrassing for you," I said to the crazy lady.

Tova sucked in her cheeks, producing a well-practiced pout. "She obviously got them from Bow Wow."

What the? I leaned forward, invading her personal bubble. She stepped back and had the presence of mind to look worried. "I don't think so. Have you considered she caught them from a dog at yoga?" I kept my tone sweet and non-confrontational.

A glance at Grey told me I wasn't as successful as I'd thought.

He cleared his throat. "Ladies, can't this wait?"

Tova picked up Kiki and pressed her wiggly body against her not-so-natural cleavage. "I was assured it didn't happen there."

I was assured it didn't happen there, I mimicked silently. "Well, I just assured you it didn't happen at Bow Wow."

By now we had an audience. Not just our small table of people. Oh no, half the room leaned in our direction, waiting for me to knock Tova on her beautiful butt.

I walked a fine line. Fleas aren't deadly, but no one would knowingly expose their pet or themselves. I clenched and unclenched my fists. What to do, what to do . . .

"Melinda, what's going on?" Mona Michaels and her Afghan Hound, Fluffy, paraded to our table.

Great. Trouble on six legs.

Mona ruled the rich and famous of Laguna Beach with the wave of her aristocratic hand and her elite American Express Black Card. She had her plastic surgeon on speed dial, injectable Botox in her purse and her private chef on a short leash.

Her simple black Valentino gown was most likely the envy of every woman at the ball. She was what the gated community housewives dreamed of being when they grew up.

Unfortunately for me, Mona and my mother were childhood friends. Mona thought that meant she could dictate, and I'd blindly follow. Not likely. I wasn't a Mona fan.

From behind, Fluffy looked exactly like her human. A mistake I'd made more than once. *Awkward.*

Tonight, Fluffy seemed more haughty than normal. Her jeweled collar with a diamond-crusted, heart-shaped pendant sparkled like a mirror ball, and I'm guessing was equally as heavy. She looked like she couldn't be bothered mingling with us average humans.

Too bad Mona didn't feel the same indifference. She narrowed her assessing blue eyes at me and waited for an explanation.

Why she thought she'd get one was beyond me.

"Go back to your posse, Mona. Everything here's just hunky-dory."

Mona motioned to the crowd; her shocking white hair flowed softly around her razor-sharp cheekbones. "It is plain to everyone you do *not* have this situation under control, otherwise Amelia wouldn't be cowering in the corner of the stage waiting for you to finish."

As always, Mona's condescending clipped voice raised my hackles.

"You may want to consider keeping your voice down," Grey warned under his breath.

Too late. All eyes had followed Mona. Once she'd insinuated herself into my business, I had my reputation to protect. I turned my attention back to Tova.

"You still haven't explained why I owe you money?"

"Well, I had to get Kiki groomed," Tova stammered. Mona's presence loomed over us, and Tova was beginning to crack. Amateur. If she wanted to make it here, she'd have to develop a thicker skin.

"And?" I could feel the weight of the room shift towards us waiting to hear the answer. Who knew dogs could be so quiet?

"My lawyer says you have to reimburse me for it."

"Oh, hell no."

Murmurs rolled through the room like Main Beach waves crashing against the rocks.

Tova stood her ground. "She got them while on your property. You have to pay," she insisted.

I hiked up my gown, which pooled around my three-inch heels. I wished I was wearing my motorcycle boots. "You're the only one with fleas." I took a breath and tried to control my rising voice and cover the Texas accent that was threatening to make an appearance. "If this was a Bow Wow issue, someone else would have said something."

"They're afraid of you," Tova whined.

"You're ridiculous," Mona pronounced with the wave of her hand.

"You're out of control," I said at the same time.

I don't know if Mona was talking to me or Tova. I was talking about both of them.

Tova shook her head. "You don't know what kind of nightmare I've been through. Kiki's wardrobe had to be dry-cleaned, my carpet steamed, her travel bag replaced, and she had to be groomed a second time after her botanical dip."

I'd had enough. "I do not have fleas!" I turned to the room, hands on hips and asked, "Did I give any of you fleas?"

There was a lot of throat clearing and minimal eye contact. No one said a word. It would have been comical if I hadn't been so honked off.

I narrowed my eyes on Tova. "Looks like it's just you."

"Enough." Mona pointed at Tova. "Take your dog and sit."

"This isn't over." Tova looked between Mona and me like a confused puppy; her shoulders sagged, and her bottom lip quivered slightly. "You'll regret pushing me around."

"Does this mean you and Kiki won't be by tomorrow to pick up the barrettes you special-ordered?"

"Melinda," Mona said, "If you know what's good for you, you'll sit and stop causing a scene."

"Don't. As much as you like to worm your way into my life, and everyone else's for that matter, you're not my mother."

Mona turned toward me. A glint of fire danced in her eyes. A chill of warning rolled down my back.

"True," she said. "Fluffy *earned* her crown. I didn't need to act like a dog in heat for the judges to see her true *talent*."

That was it. The woman insulted me and my Mama.

Bitter emotion churned until it turned into a roar of fury. I yanked my wine glass from the table and tossed the deep ruby contents on Mona's dress. Immediately, I knew I'd crossed the line. The fat was in the fire now.

Grey groaned in disappointment. Missy jumped out from under the table and barked, her crown rolling under my chair.

Everyone else was deathly silent.

Mona stood frozen, her hands in the air.

Then suddenly she hissed. "You fool."

Fluffy tossed her pale tresses from her eyes and snarled.

The room erupted into chaos. People jumped up from their seats. They talked over each other, shocked, yet lapping up the juicy gossip of my behavior.

The dogs barked, Missy included. Canines turned on each other and their humans. Leashes wrapped around chairs, tables, and human legs, dragging everything behind them in their excitement.

"Don't touch me," Mona ordered to a handful of dimwits who thought they'd get into her good graces by mopping the wine from her dress.

I dropped to my knees to retrieve Missy's crown.

"If you'd like to use the ladies room, I'd be happy to keep an eye on Fluffy," Grey offered, his calm voice sounding out-of-place amidst the pandemonium.

I got to my feet, Missy's leash in one hand her crown in the other.

Mona yanked the white cloth napkin Grey held out for her. She patted her dress as if taking a public wine bath was an everyday occurrence. "If you don't leave now, I'll call the police and have you arrested." She quickly found her normal condescending voice.

I couldn't believe what I was hearing. "Are you kidding me? You deserved it. Everyone knows it." I gestured toward the group of gawkers.

"Melinda, you've done enough." Grey's tone was tense and didn't hold room for disagreement.

I whipped around. "You're taking her side?" I felt like I'd been stabbed in the heart.

"No, I'm trying to keep you from going to jail," he muttered.

I snagged my gold clutch from the table and shoved Missy's crown on my head. Tears burned my eyes. "I'm sorry I've embarrassed you."

I meant it. I was sorry. Of course, that didn't change the fact that I'd just acted like an idiot. My snap judgment was in full throttle. Once in gear, it was difficult to apply the brakes.

He grabbed my arm and stopped my dramatic exit. "This isn't about me." He jerked his head toward the back of the room.

Caro looked like I'd just kicked her dog, Dogbert. Her face had turned the same color as the vintage red satin gown she wore. Her tightened lips formed a straight line and her snappy green eyes had narrowed into angry slits. Sam Gallanos, her date, stood silently at her side, his dark eyes studying me.

I'd forgotten all about Caro. I'd blindly embraced my anger and had completely lost sight of the fundraising goal for the Fur Ball.

Intense self-reproach latched onto my heart and squeezed. I wish I could say it was an unfamiliar feeling. But I couldn't.

I guided Missy through the mayhem with only one purpose in mind—to confront the only thing standing between me and a hasty exit so I could berate my lack of judgment in private.

"I didn't plan on making a scene," I said to my cousin. It was as close to an apology as I could manage at the moment.

Caro eyed the crown. Then the brooch.

Anyone else would have looked away and ignored me, casting me to social purgatory. Instead, her eyes locked onto mine, and she said, "You never do, sugar."

I couldn't argue. I'd left her one hell of a mess to clean up.

"You'll need to call Nigel," Caro's soft southern accent hung on the family lawyer's name.

I covered the brooch protectively with my hand.

"Are you fixin' to sue me, cousin?" I asked, unable to keep the Texas out of my voice.

She shook her head and looked at me like I'd hopped on the crazy train, which apparently I had.

"Geeze Louise, Mel. You just humiliated Mona in public. You know she won't let you get away with it."

Chapter Three

After my outrageous behavior last night (yes, I admit I behaved badly), my shop was *the* place to be seen. It was crazy.

Melinda, the lead you sold me clashes with Chopper's new outfit. I must *have a new one. Melinda, why didn't you tell me gold leather carriers are all the rage? Melinda, do you have more diamond-crusted collars? Can I special-order a pink mink snuggie?*

And on it went. My clients were addicted to their dogs (and gossip). It was obvious their lives revolved around their pooches and their accessories. I loved the business, but it was exhausting.

If someone with significant height on the society ladder showed an interest in an accessory, I suddenly couldn't keep it in stock. Everyone wanted what someone else had. The Oprah effect for pampered pet bling.

"Melinda, do you have the Prada collar in cantaloupe? Orange makes Diesel sad," a newer customer asked.

I glanced at Diesel, a deaf Dalmatian. He looked outlandish in his Swarovski crystal sport coat and star-shaped sunglasses. He sparkled, shimmered and reflected with every shake. Trust me, the orange leather studded collar was the least of his worries. Diesel and his human needed some beauty queen intervention.

"Sorry, no cantaloupe. Try this." I grabbed a flat-gold leather Prada collar instead. "Gold makes everyone happy."

"Perfect." She clapped her hands in delight, then deftly fastened the collar around Diesel's skinny neck. "I'll take two."

I smiled at her enthusiasm. "Great."

The door opened, and Mona Michaels strolled inside. Dark sunglasses, cream Chanel pantsuit, and a cloud of expensive perfume. No Fluffy.

In the chaos of the day, I'd forgotten all about Mona and the inevitable wrath I'd experience. Caro had hit it on the nose; Mona would extract revenge.

Tricia Edwards, Mona's best friend and business partner, followed behind, carrying a sample case. The two were thick as fleas on a coonhound and just as irritating.

Tricia designed dog wear, but didn't own a dog because they were messy. (That didn't make sense to me, either.) Mona was the money behind Tricia's label. The two had been badgering me for months to carry Tricia's couture dog dresses. I'd finally agreed to meet with them next week to look at the inventory. I wasn't holding out much hope.

"Melinda, I have a new selection of samples for you." Tricia's frosty voice cut through the fevered shopping chatter.

"Bring them to the meeting next week," I said without giving either of them my full attention.

I gently wrapped Diesel's second collar and rang up the sale. I slipped a couple of dog treats in the bag before handing it over. "I hope Diesel enjoys his new bling."

His owner smiled broadly. "We will. Thanks. You're still coming to Diesel's Bark-mitzvah, right?"

"Absolutely. I wouldn't miss it," I promised.

"I'll see you then." Her smile faltered slightly as she brushed past Tricia and Mona.

"Mona's unexpectedly free today," Tricia pressed, setting her case on the counter. "You're going to love them." Her pushy excitement rang hollow in my ears.

"I'm swamped. Next week."

I grabbed a box from behind the counter and headed for the front display case. I pulled out a handful of pink Juicy Couture collars with rhinestone charms from the packing material and restocked the shelves, keeping my back to the self-appointed mayors of Laguna Beach.

"Melinda, what are you wearing?" Mona's haughty voice hung in the air like a guilty verdict thrust on an innocent man.

I took inventory of my typical work outfit. Black leather vest over my "Paws off!" t-shirt, motorcycle boots and, my most recent splurge, a pair of True Religion jeans. Even my hair was pulled back into a long sleek ponytail and out of my face.

"You have something against Yorkies?" I asked as I turned around.

"You've embroidered them on your . . ." Mona waved her sunglasses at my butt.

"You'd have preferred them somewhere else?"

"It's silly," she said.

"Not everyone's bound by what others deem inappropriate." Darby Beckett, my best friend for the last two years, closed in ranks behind me.

Unlike last night's crowd, Darby represented the small faction of Laguna residents who don't have piles of money. Originally from Nebraska, she didn't always relate to the west coast shenanigans.

Darby owned Paw Prints, the pet photography shop next door. She'd had a last minute cancellation, and she'd graciously offered to pop over and help me with the mad crush of customers. God love her. Darby had the same Mona-chip on her shoulder as I did. Maybe even bigger.

Mona looked right past Darby. "Melinda, your mother would be appalled to see you dressed in secondhand throwaways."

I sighed. Mona had me on that one. Mama would be aghast at my typical attire. "Where's Fluffy?" I asked.

"Cliff has her," Tricia said.

Cliff Michaels was Mona's fourth ex-husband. They shared custody of Fluffy.

Fluffy wasn't your average Afghan. She was a dog actor. In the past few years, she'd won two Daytime Emmys for a guest role on a soap opera. She'd played a Lassie type, saving the resident drama queen from drowning. Maybe the soap would still be on the air today if they'd have killed her off. The drama queen, not Fluffy. Never kill the dog.

Cliff, on the other hand, seemed like a nice enough guy, but after two years of marriage he'd had enough of Mona and had left their multi-million dollar mansion for a "modest" yacht he'd named *Ruthless* (Mona's middle name was Ruth). Last I'd heard he'd docked the boat at Dana Point Marina, about twenty minutes south.

"Melinda, we have business to attend to. I don't have all day," Mona insisted.

I took a deep breath, well aware I couldn't afford a repeat of last night.

"Mona, I have customers to assist. I will meet with you next week. Like we agreed." One look around the shop, and anyone could see that my customers weren't blazin' a trail to pay up and leave behind the free entertainment.

"You don't really want to cross me. Do you?" Mona tilted her head. Not much. Just enough to make her face look more intimidating than normal.

"We're not afraid of you." Darby's bouncy blond curls slapped the side of her face. She stood next to me in an attempt to give the illusion of a united front.

Mona's shrewd eyes locked on her. "You should be my little rabbit."

Darby sucked in a sharp breath. She opened and closed her mouth, but no words came out. Her small frame vibrated in what I assumed was panic and anger. I squeezed my best friend's hand.

"Mona, leave Darby out of this." I kept my voice low, trying my darnedest to not make a scene. "If you have something to say to me, say it. Otherwise, get out."

Darby wagged her finger at Mona, not willing to back down. "Some day, you'll get what what's coming to you."

I could have sworn Mona stiffened, but it was hard to tell since she was already so unyielding.

Tricia stuffed her phone inside her Marc Jacobs bag and looked at Mona for their next move. We all waited.

Mona didn't disappoint.

"When you continue to humiliate people in public, the only way for them to save face is to sue," Mona slipped her sunglasses into the protective case.

"Sounds like you're speaking from experience." Sue for what? Geez Louise. I didn't have patience for mind games.

Mona casually adjusted her purse strap, and then thrust the figurative dagger into my back and twisted. "I called your mother last night. Babs and I had a wonderful time catching up. I talked her into coming out for a visit."

I wasn't afraid of Mona, but I was absolutely avoiding my mother (for the record, no one called Barbara Langston "Babs" to her face). I love my Mama, but she left me dog-tired.

"I'm sure you left out the part where you called her a prostitute," I said. I had every right to be upset at my Mama, but for an outsider to insult her (and anyone who's not family is just that, an outsider), was unacceptable.

I heard a soft gasp. I looked around the shop. There were at least five customers pretending to study the merchandise.

Mona shrugged. "I did no such thing. Besides, Barbara has moved past that."

Just because Mama didn't talk about *The Incident*, didn't mean she was over it. She was southern. One didn't air their dirty laundry in private. Let alone in public. Mona, on the other hand, didn't have a problem dressing-down anyone in front of an audience. The bigger the scandal, the happier she seemed.

She had zero southern manners.

"We agreed. You owe me an apology. A *public* apology," Mona continued, condemning me with every word and savoring every second.

"I hope you didn't get your stone-heart set on that apology," I said.

"You wouldn't want to damage her reputation any more than you already have, would you, dear?"

Her arrogant tone choked me like a Texas heat wave in the middle of August. It took all the resolve I possessed to control my temper. "Get. Out."

Tricia's eyes widened in shock. "You can't kick us out." Her voice trembled.

"I just did."

Mona's eyebrow rose in warning. "You'll regret this."

Cold anger oozed through my body and settled in all the wrong places, making me say and do all the wrong things. Again. Some day I'd figure it out. But that wasn't today. Mona had crossed the line.

"You're a bitter selfish woman. I don't cotton to threats against my family or my friends. The only thing I regret is that I didn't take y'all down last night when I had the chance."

Chapter Four

Sometimes I find myself on the brink of trouble without trying. It was doubtful I'd "regret" ordering Mona and her lap dog, Tricia, out of Bow Wow. Although I had to admit, I hadn't thought through what I'd meant by "take you down." That was an unfortunate choice of words.

I'd like to report Mona and Tricia had immediately skedaddled, but that's not how it played out. They'd split on their terms—right after Mona had received an "urgent" call from the pet psychic, Josephine "Jo" O'Malley.

My loyal customers had been all abuzz about how I'd stood up to Mona—half proud, the other half worried about the repercussions. Their concern was unexpected, touching and probably warranted.

God bless Darby, she'd had my back the whole time and stuck around until the last customers had toted their purchases out the door. Darby was top dog in my book.

It was three o'clock, and I was starving. I locked the shop to woof down a late lunch. I'd just swallowed a mouthful of turkey and avocado sandwich when Darby pounded on Bow Wow's front door. I dropped my food on the counter and scrambled to let her in, my boots squeaking on the hardwood floor.

I swung the door open, and the salty ocean breeze rushed inside. "I wasn't expecting to see you again."

Darby swept past me, looking very Annie Leibovitz in her black button-up shirt and jeans.

"I'm not alone," she said.

Sixty pounds of sleek muscle trailed behind her. Fluffy.

"Where in Sam Hill did she come from?" I choked out, shutting the door behind them.

Fluffy paused next to the Louis Vuitton dog carriers and shook. Stray fur and a handful of leaves landed on the throw rug. She blithely scanned the empty shop, nose and tail in the air.

That dog had more attitude than an Orange County teenager.

"I was propping my 'I'm next door' sign in the window, when

Cliff's Land Rover sped by. That's when I noticed Fluffy."

Unfortunately, this wasn't the first time Cliff had ditched Fluffy at my boutique. A while back, he'd petitioned the court for a neutral meeting point, arguing Mona's mansion was a hostile environment. The judge had decided that, for the welfare of the dog, the hand-over had to happen at a place familiar to Fluffy, but not at either residence. I don't think the judge meant Bow Wow.

"Come here, girl," I called out.

Fluffy's dark almond-shaped eyes regarded me skeptically. The aloof expression she carried so effortlessly was firmly in place. With a shake of her head, she strutted to my office in the back. If history was an indicator, she was headed for Missy's dog bed.

"Good thing Missy's home." Unsure of how the day's events would unfold, I'd left her at the house where she could sleep in peace.

Darby and I plopped onto the stools behind the counter. She tossed her keys next to my water bottle and snagged a salt 'n vinegar chip. She popped it in her mouth and immediately made a sour face. I slid the bag closer to her. The sound of our crunching chips filled the silence.

"I thought Cliff only had Fluffy on Wednesdays and every other weekend?" Darby asked. "It's Monday."

"That's what I thought, too. Hey, about earlier. Mona got a little crazy. Are you okay?" I asked.

She shrugged. "I'm fine. What about you?" Concern shadowed her delicate features.

"I'm relieved they finally left. Thanks for sticking around. You didn't need to, but I really appreciate it."

She bumped her shoulder against mine. "That's what best friends do. So . . . guess who my last-minute client is." Darby's blue eyes sparkled with mischief.

"Male or female?" I loved this game. Darby's popularity was growing, and in a tight-knit community like Laguna, that translated into loyal customers.

Before she could answer, the door flew open and Jo O'Malley, pet psychic extraordinaire, burst inside. The smell of motorcycle exhaust and burnt dog treats trailed behind her.

Her tangled red hair whipped her face, causing her to look like she'd just gone ten rounds with a paddle brush and can of hair spray. And lost.

"Her?" I asked under my breath while giving Darby the what-were-you-thinking look. "You're a *pet photographer*."

"She talks to animals." Darby wiped her salt-covered fingers on her jeans and then hopped off the stool. "Close enough for me."

Jo didn't exactly fit the stereotypical idea of what a pet psychic looked like. You know, they were either all-business or bohemian gypsy. She was one hundred percent a motorcycle chick.

Her wrinkled black tank top was partially tucked into the front of her torn jeans. And not the kind of jeans you'd buy torn. She'd come by *those* rips honestly.

I couldn't badmouth her motorcycle boots since I was currently wearing the same ones. But the humongous Lassie tattoo on her upper left arm . . . well, that just made me smile.

"Do you think Lassie barks when there's trouble?" I asked, quietly.

Darby coughed back a giggle and shot me a look meant to keep me quiet. She snatched the keys to her studio, then met Jo next to the display of small dog sweaters and dresses.

"Thanks for getting me in at the last minute," Jo's raspy voice reverberated throughout the quiet shop. "I normally get those free ones online. I thought I'd go for a more professional look. You know, now that business has picked up."

Oh. My. Lord. It took all my will power not to roll my eyes. She wouldn't know professional if it was a Doberman Pinscher and it bit her in the butt.

"No problem," Darby said. "There's a dressing room at Paw Prints if you'd like to change."

Jo looked herself over. "Change into what?"

Darby had her hands full with this one. I slid off the stool and joined them, curious about the emergency call earlier this afternoon.

"Congratulations. I couldn't help but overhear that your business is doing well," I said to Jo.

She frowned, making her look much older than her thirty-years. "You sound surprised. Doesn't everyone want to understand their pet?"

I was hard pressed to take her seriously. In my humble opinion, she was nuttier than a fruitcake. Once, she'd told me Missy chewed a pair of strappy Marc Jacobs heels because she didn't feel pretty. Missy (her papered name is Miss Congeniality) has won her share of ugliest bulldog contests and is well aware she's "unattractive." Let's not even bring up her hideous under bite. It didn't take a pet psychic to know Missy had chewed my heels because I'd left them on the bedroom floor, and she was *bored.*

"I'm not surprised," I said, "but I am curious as to what constitutes an emergency pet reading?"

She blinked twice, then narrowed her eyes and assessed me. I'd spent enough time around "users" and "haters" to recognize that gleam in her eyes. She was looking for my weaknesses.

"What do you mean?" she asked.

"I'm sure Mel didn't mean anything," Darby said quickly, her eyes sending me a silent message.

I automatically produced my beauty pageant smile meant to inspire trust and reassurance. Darby shook her head. She wasn't voting for me.

I returned my attention to Jo. "Mona was here when you called. I didn't realize you could have a reading without the pet."

Her face softened and became almost ethereal. "They don't need to be present in order for me to have an accurate reading. I tune into the animals' energy."

I wondered if she was tuning into my energy. It screamed *phony*. Fluffy currently snoozed away in my backroom, and Jo The Magnificent hadn't picked up on a thing.

"So you'd be able to tune into Fluffy's 'energy' from here, no matter where she was?"

Jo tilted her head to the side, her eyelids flittering as she spoke. "Fluffy's energy is very dynamic. If she wanted to tell me something, I would know."

"Like this afternoon?" I asked.

"My appointments are confidential. I will tell you this much. Fluffy came to me in a dream. To warn me. I was obligated to tell Mona. Any decent person would have done the same." Gone was the light airy tone. Her foghorn voice was back in control, and the Lassie tattoo growled.

Well, okay then.

Jo turned and slithered toward the door. "Let's go, Darby. I have an appointment this evening."

I had more questions than answers. That wasn't going to change anytime soon.

Chapter Five

Mona was missing.

Not kidnapped missing. Missing as in, the boutique closed in ten minutes, and you-know-who was still roaming through the shop. I'd left two voicemails for Mona and hadn't heard a word. I didn't like where this was heading.

Fluffy had decided to grace me with her presence and was shoving her pointy nose in my merchandise and sniffing loudly.

"Come on, Fluffy. Give it a rest. Wanna Bowser Treat?" I pulled a biscuit out of the jar by the register and waved it in her direction. She scrutinized me in her regal disposition, unimpressed.

The front door opened and Don Furry, an ARL volunteer, entered.

"Hey, Don," I greeted. "How's it going?"

He waved hello. "Fine. Just fine. I thought I'd stop in and see if you had—" He stopped in his tracks. "Th-that's Mona's dog."

"Sure is." I dropped the treat back into the jar.

"Is *she* here?" he asked in a nervous whisper.

I shook my head, slightly amused at his odd reaction. "Nope. Fluffy's officially a stray."

He blinked, puzzled. "Fluffy's not a stray."

"Okay, she's been abandoned." Fluffy casually sauntered over to Don and me. She sniffed Don's pants and then sneezed twice. She looked up at me and, I swear, if she had an eyebrow, it'd be arched.

Don's eyes practically popped out of his head.

I really wanted to laugh, but I could see Don was not amused at Fluffy's antics. "She's an actor. Those were probably fake sneezes. What can I do for you?"

"I, ah, I stopped by to pick up the towels you said you'd set aside for the ARL." He hadn't taken his eyes off Fluffy.

I'd forgotten all about the donation. "I've got the box in the backroom. I'll be right back. Would you keep an eye on the dog? She's been sticking her nose where it doesn't belong."

I was gone about a minute and returned with a large cardboard box filled with linens. "I threw in some sheets and blankets, too."

"Thanks, Mel. So, what are you going to do with . . ." He nodded toward Fluffy.

I shrugged. "I don't know. You want to take her back to the ARL with you?" I teased.

He held up his hands, his clean shaven face pale. "We don't have room."

"Since when?"

"Today." His bald head glistened with beads of sweat.

"Okay, spill it. What's going on?"

"We really are full. Did you hear about the puppy mill raid? We took in twenty-six dogs a couple of days ago."

That wasn't the whole story. I'd never heard Don turn away a dog. "What aren't you saying?"

He checked his watch, then looked around as if he was about to disclose a national secret. "Mona's our biggest benefactor. Every year, following the Fur Ball, she makes her largest contribution. If I take Fluffy, it could cost the ARL millions. *MILLIONS*. I can't take that chance."

He was right. Mona was spiteful enough to punish the ARL because of some perceived slight. "It's okay, Don. I was just teasing you," I said. "I'll take care of Her Highness. Don't worry about a thing. I've got it all under control."

Chapter Six

The only thing I had under control was my wardrobe.

I'd left Mona a third voicemail. Still no callback. I'd called Darby, asking her to drop by my place to let Missy out while I dealt with Fluffy. You guessed it—I got her voicemail, too. I left a message and crossed my fingers that she'd hear it sooner rather than later.

I could have picked up Missy myself, but I didn't want to subject her to a Mona tirade for drooling on the marble foyer. There were some hygiene problems a girl just couldn't help.

Getting Fluffy into the Jeep was easier in theory than action. She's one stubborn dog, but we finally came to an understanding.

I pointed the Jeep south on Pacific Coast Highway (PCH to the locals). With the top off, every once in a while I could hear the crashing waves. I lowered the visor, blocking the glare of blushing pink swirls and the blaze of brilliant orange streaking the sky. I sighed in contentment. Another spectacular evening in paradise.

I made my way to the prestigious gated community, Sapphire Bay. Being rich wasn't enough to live on the other side of the iron gate. You had to be vetted, sponsored and have more money than God.

I rolled to a stop next to the security shack. Mr. Rent-A-Cop stuck his head out the window. He was on the downhill side of middle-aged with a bushy gray mustache. Faded green eyes scrutinized us through his bifocals. He recognized Fluffy right away. I, on the other hand, got a complete once over, including a raised unibrow.

"Name," he asked, completely unimpressed I had Mona's dog.

"Melinda Langston."

He reviewed the clipboard in his hand. Non-residents didn't just waltz thought the hallowed entrance. Someone had to authorize your visit. I was ninety-nine percent sure I wasn't on "the list."

I slid him a beauty queen smile and fibbed like a five-year-old. "Mona had an unexpected emergency and asked me to bring Fluffy home. She assured me she'd let someone know I was coming."

He tucked his clipboard under his arm. "Sorry."

I eyed him, considering my next move. "I guess you're right. I certainly wouldn't want you to do anything that might get you into trouble." I put the Jeep in neutral and pulled up the emergency brake. "I'll just leave Fluffy with you. I'll let Mona know where to pick her up."

He grunted. Looking past his skepticism and the community rules, he let us through the gate.

I followed the smattering of wispy palm trees to Mona's oceanfront mansion. I pulled into the circular drive and parked next to the fountain.

"Let me refresh your memory on the Mel-Rules. I'm the human. No gloating. No dragging. Got it?"

Fluffy pawed at the door and whined.

"Good grief. Let me grab my bag and cell."

Unlike the dog, I wasn't in a big hurry. The last person I wanted to see was Mona. If I was lucky, the housekeeper, Camilla, would open the door and take Fluffy off my hands.

I went around to the passenger side and opened the door. I attached the leash to Fluffy's diamond-studded collar and released her from the safety belt. The second I stepped back, the crazy dog jumped out and dragged me toward the multi-story Mediterranean-style home.

So much for the rules. Fluffy could use a visit from a pet therapist I knew. Once we reached the front door, Fluffy stopped and looked at me expectantly.

"*Hello?* I'm the human. I thought we had an agreement?" I could tell from her expression she didn't care about what I was saying. She wanted in. I wanted to go home. I rang the bell.

Cathedral-style bells filled the inside of the house. Okay, it wasn't really church bells, but it could have been. I looked down at Fluffy, who didn't seem at all bothered by the flamboyance.

"Really? This is what you come home to every day?"

We waited. No one came.

I rang the bell again.

Bong. Bong. Bong. Bong. Bong.

Just shoot me now. Please.

We continued to wait.

Fluffy grew more restless with each passing second, which made me equally antsy. Having the dog was a perfectly legitimate reason to walk inside, but my southern manners dictated I wait for someone to invite me in. Well, that and the security system.

I pounded on the door. Fluffy continued to whine and paw. Still, no one came. Forget manners. Forget the alarm. I tried the door.

Unbelievably, it swung open. And there was no screeching alarm.

"Wow." I glanced behind me before I took a couple of steps. As soon as my foot hit the marble entryway, Fluffy lunged forward, taking me for another drag. She stopped in the middle of an ornate foyer bigger than my entire living room and kitchen combined.

"Hello? Anyone home?" My voice echoed in the empty silence.

I expected the housekeeper to appear any second. "Camilla? Mona?"

Fluffy strained against the leash as she edged her way toward the stairs. The moment I unhooked her, she charged up the curved oak staircase leading to what I assumed was her wing of the house. I waited for Mona to make her trademark entrance, descending the staircase like a classic Hollywood actress ready for her close-up, but she was a no-show.

Then it hit me, Mona was probably at Bow Wow. Her Jag wasn't in the drive, although it could be in the garage. It would be just like Mona to come when it was convenient for her.

I quickly pulled my cell from my purse and punched in her number. Within seconds a cell phone rang behind me. I spun around. Mona's phone was on the hall table.

I grabbed it. "That's not good."

I ended the call, absently dumping the phones in my purse, and then dropping it on the hall table.

"Mona," I called out louder. Where the heck was she? I couldn't leave Fluffy behind until I knew Mona was home. Good grief, she better not have taken a spontaneous trip to the Caymans.

I climbed the stairs two at a time. "Mona. I've delivered your dog."

Fluffy poked her head around the corner and barked as I reached the top of the stairs.

I jumped back. It was the first time I'd heard her bark without a cue. Or a camera.

"What's gotten into you?"

Fluffy planted her feet and barked again.

"I'm not allowed up here?"

Her dark eyes bored into mine, then she quickly turned and trotted down the hallway.

"Oh, now I speak dog," I muttered.

I bought her Lassie act and followed. We zigged through hallways, zagged past a half dozen rooms, and I wondered if I should've left a trail of bread crumbs. Finally Fluffy stopped in front of a closed door, looking more exasperated than usual.

I rolled my eyes. Lord, she was demanding. "All that barking because you can't get to your throne?"

I opened the door. She pushed past me and sniffed around. I took a quick peek and realized it was Mona's bedroom.

Being more than a little curious, I left my southern manners in the hallway and allowed myself a quick look. I was immediately drawn to the beautiful oil canvas of an Italian river sunset hanging at the head of her king sized bed. The blush colored duvet cost more than my brand new Jeep.

Way too much white, gold and fringe for my taste, but it fit Mona perfectly. A beautiful tall armless chair was precisely positioned in the corner. I could easily imagine Mona lounging aristocratically, Fluffy at her feet. It was all very old Hollywood.

My eye was drawn to the dozens of framed photos of Fluffy. On the beach, at a dog show, on the set of *The Guiding Lighthouse*, Fluffy with Julia Roberts. (Okay, I had to do a double take on that one. I swear to the Lord Almighty, Fluffy's hair was styled exactly like Julia's. They were *twins.*)

I turned to leave and stopped in my tracks. Right above the fireplace hung a life-sized gilded-framed painting of the dynamic duo—side-by-side, matching hair color and aristocratic expressions, with Mona's arm draped over Fluffy's back. The adoration on Mona's face was obvious. The painting was beautiful and, at the same time, a little creepy.

Mona loved Fluffy. No, Mona worshipped Fluffy. She'd never abandon her dog.

Something was wrong. Why would Mona leave her front door unlocked, the alarm off and her cell phone behind?

Fluffy shoved me out of her way and trotted down the hallway to the next room. Once again, I followed. Certainly, whatever was behind door number two would be equally draped in luxurious excess and might give a clue to Mona's whereabouts.

I'd barely turned the knob when Fluffy barged past me, head-butting the door against the wall with a loud bang.

I stumbled through the doorway. It wasn't a room. It was a mini-palace fit for a movie star. Fluffy's palace. A white sheepskin rug in front of her personal fireplace, a king-sized sleigh bed and a dressing screen (why a dog needed a dressing screen was beyond me). Fresh filtered water dripped into her Wedgewood doggie bowl.

It was also a disaster.

Fluffy's wardrobe was strewn throughout the room, draped precariously on the bed, and hanging out of open drawers. While Mona had an obscene amount of photos, Fluffy had her own slew of trophies and ribbons. All of them haphazardly tossed about.

The room looked like it had been ransacked.

Fluffy disappeared behind the disheveled bed. Her tail stopped wagging and she whined softly.

That's when I saw her.

At first, I wasn't certain what I was looking at. Then it became clear. Mona was sprawled on the floor as if posing for a men's magazine. It was almost picture perfect, except for the blood matting her five hundred dollar haircut and the gold statue stuck in her head.

I hesitantly moved closer. Fluffy nuzzled Mona's cheek. When she didn't move, Fluffy pawed her shoulder, still whining.

"I don't think she's getting up, girl," I said softly.

Mona was dead. Deader than a stuffed Poodle.

Chapter Seven

Right after I'd dialed 9-1-1, I called the one person I trusted to tell me what to do next.

"Someone whacked Mona with Fluffy's Emmy." The words tumbled out of my mouth the second Grey had said hello.

"Are you injured?" he asked, voice thick with concern.

"No, just wigged out."

"Where are you?"

I paced the length of the hallway between Fluffy and Mona's room. "I'm still at Mona's. This is my first dead body, and I have to tell you, it's not like what you see on TV. I think I'm going to puke."

"Hold on, I'm on my way." He was in his secret FBI mode. Gone was the art dealer persona he carried for cover. His normal teasing tone had transformed into solid, calm and controlled.

"Mona would *die* if she knew people were going to see her like this." I cringed at my bad choice of words, but it was true.

I could hear Mona's bored monotone voice ordering me to pull the statue out of her head and clean up the mess before it stained her one-of-a-kind hardwood floor. Once the room had been cleaned to her satisfaction, she'd demand her hair and makeup touched-up before any crime scene photos were snapped.

It was the God's honest truth. That was just Mona's way.

And after what I'd seen, I can't say I'd blame her. Speaking of cleaning up, where *was* Camilla?

"Mona's one bloody mess," I said.

Papers rustled on the other end of the line as Grey cleared his desk. "Don't touch her," he said. His deep timber instilled a calmness I needed.

"I didn't." I poked my head into the room. I cupped the bottom of the phone and whispered, "The dog's covered in blood and won't leave Mona."

"If you need help, call Caro."

"I can handle Fluffy." The sick smell of blood was a different matter. I breathed through my mouth and willed my stomach to stop churning. I heard a car door slam and an engine start over the phone. He was on his way.

"Don't move. Better yet, wait outside for the police. Don't touch anything. Don't talk to anyone. I'll be there in fifteen minutes."

In that mess, I doubted the cops would notice if I touched anything. Outside sirens screamed through the dignified gated community.

"You'd better hurry. The cavalry's almost here," I said.

We ended our call, and I realized I was shaking so badly I looked like I'd downed a case of energy drinks.

I shook my head trying to erase the scene on the other side of the wall. But Mona's image was branded in my mind.

I methodically inched through the hallway maze, really wishing for those bread crumbs. By the time I'd made it down the stairs, I'd stopped shaking and was once again a nose breather.

I opened the front door and inhaled the fresh air. The Pacific had never smelled so good. After a minute of gathering myself, I made my way back inside, leaving the door open, an invitation for the police. I sank to the bottom step of the staircase and waited for the troops.

They didn't rush inside guns drawn like on the TV dramas, but they didn't stroll in like it was a Saturday open house either. Brawny and carrying an air of authority that wouldn't be overlooked, four uniformed officers entered. Two paused directly in front of me, while the other pair searched the downstairs.

Wasn't four cops a little overkill? The police must have been on high alert after Kevin Blackstone's murder.

"Are you injured?" Cop Number One asked.

Question of the day.

I shook my head. I was having a difficult time finding my voice. I wasn't as together as I'd thought.

His blue eyes assessed me and our immediate surroundings. His short cropped brown hair reminded me of my cousin, Wyatt, on my daddy's side. Wyatt didn't think girls could do anything but cook, have babies, and look pretty. I didn't like Wyatt.

I had no idea what Cop Number One thought as he processed my typical attire of motorcycle boots, faded jeans, and t-shirt.

He mumbled into the radio he wore like a tie. Someone squawked back something that only a fellow police officer, or a fast food employee, could decipher.

"Is there anyone else in the house?" Cop Number Two, who

couldn't be a day over twenty-one asked. I pegged him as the "good cop." Dark hair, dark eyes, strong jaw line and plenty of who-gives-a-crap-what-you-think attitude. To say he was "nice" was an exaggeration, but he didn't look at me as if I was already *the* prime suspect.

"No. She's upstairs, to the right. I don't remember which room but you can't miss it. It's a mess. I think I left the door open. Watch out for the dog. She's standing guard." Once I'd found my voice I rambled, offering random details.

With a nod of acknowledgment, the third and fourth cops walked past us and headed upstairs.

"What kind of dog?" Cop Number One was back.

He had to be kidding. There was someone in Laguna who didn't know Mona and her four-legged sidekick? "I thought everyone knew Mona and Fluffy."

"Which one's the dog?" Cop Number One pulled out his black notebook.

It wasn't a completely brainless question. There were many women named "Fluffy" in Orange County. But the fact that he didn't know who Mona Michaels or Fluffy were made him Dumbo Cop.

"Fluffy."

"Call the vet," Dumbo Cop said to his partner. "I'm not going to get bit by some diva dog." He jammed his notebook in his front shirt pocket.

"What are you going to do?" I hopped up from the stairs, slightly blocking his path.

"Who are you?" he asked, clearly annoyed.

"Melinda Langston. I'm the one who found Mona and called 9-1-1. Why do you need a vet?"

"We may need to tranquilize the dog if he—"

"She."

"What?" He pinned me down with a stare meant to shake my confidence.

"Fluffy's a she. And you can't drug her. I'll call my cousin, she's a pet shrink."

"You," he pointed at me, "won't call anyone."

"Caro wouldn't like being referred to as 'anyone'."

The muscle in his cheek twitched. "Who's your cousin?" His tone suggested he already knew the answer.

"Carolina Lamont. She recently solved Kevin Blackstone's murder.

You've probably met her."

His face turned red, like he popped an artery. "Sit down." He jabbed his finger at the bottom stair and then mumbled into his radio tie again. His words were incoherent, but his tone was unmistakably pissed off.

Heck, I wasn't happy I'd coughed up her name either, but she had solved Kevin's murder and cleared Diana's name in the process. More importantly, she knew dogs.

That's when Grey showed up, dressed in his dark-blue Tom Ford suit surrounded by his own air of authority. Our eyes met, and a spark of intense understanding flashed between us, striking me to the core.

Feelings of reassurance and strength washed over me; I struggled to keep back the tears.

"Are you okay?" he asked as I rushed across the foyer and into his open arms.

I nodded into his chest, hiding my weakness from him. "Better than Mona. I forgot I wasn't supposed to talk to anyone."

I felt his chest rumble with a strained laugh. "I'm not surprised."

I allowed myself to soak up everything he offered before I pulled away and led him to the French doors that opened to the sunroom.

He squeezed my shoulders and quickly took in the scene. I knew he was doing his own assessment of the situation. He was on full alert, FBI stance, absorbing and analyzing details. My chest tightened with pride. This was why I had called him. If only it didn't scare the bejeezus out of me at the same time.

Grey's green eyes fixed on the police officers talking in hushed tones. "They're not happy."

I followed his gaze. It would only be seconds before they interrogated Grey.

"A hundred bucks they think you're my attorney." I smiled as I hugged the truth. I had my very own James Bond.

Grey studied Dumbo Cop. "What did you say to him?"

I shrugged my shoulders, totally baffled at the question. "What makes you think I said anything?"

"I recognize the pained look."

I had no idea what he was talking about. When I looked at the police, all I could read on their faces was cagey suspicion.

"I offered to call Caro. Like you suggested," I reminded him.

"And . . . ?"

"And nothing." I crossed my arms and looked up into his rugged face. I was no match for his six-foot-three-inches. "I'm totally offended by what you're implying."

Grey didn't say anything with words. He let the I-know-you-better-than-that look do his talking. It was annoying.

"He didn't recognize Caro's name so I ever so gently reminded him that she'd solved Kevin's murder," I explained in the same tone I'd used to recite the grocery list to Missy as we'd walk to Whole Foods.

He actually smiled and the laugh lines around his mouth deepened into mini craters. His eyes warmed and instantly drew me in.

"You named dropped," he whispered and reached for my left hand, fingering my engagement ring. "Then you rubbed it in his face that a civilian was a major contributor in solving a murder."

"I did no such thing."

The truth of Grey's words sank in. I pulled back and narrowed my eyes. "If you tell Caro, I'll deny it."

He hugged me quickly and chuckled into my hair. "There's nothing wrong with being proud of your cousin."

"So you've told me."

The police joined us, notebooks at the ready, expressions aiming for neutral but missing the mark and landing closer to distrust. "Who are you?" Dumbo Cop asked.

"Grey Donovan. I'm Melinda's fiancé. She phoned me after calling you. I'm just making sure she's okay." He held out his hand in that boy's club way, insinuating he was only there because of me.

I could see the suspicion behind their eyes battle the desire to believe they could take Grey at face value. It was clear they didn't trust him. They shouldn't.

Grey, on the other hand, remained relaxed and at ease, patiently waiting, drawing them into his web of trust. Damn, he was good.

Eventually, Dumbo Cop accepted Grey's outstretched hand. Maybe instinct told him Grey was one of the good guys. Maybe they were just playing their own game of cat and mouse.

"Ms. Langston, do you have any idea who might want to hurt Ms. Michaels?" Dumbo Cop asked.

"Everyone in town."

He looked up from his notebook. "Isn't that a slight exaggeration?" he asked dryly.

I shook my head. "At some point, everyone in town has probably threatened Mona for some reason or another."

I caught Grey silently telling me to stop talking.

I tried to fix what I'd already started, "But to kill her? I don't think anyone hated her that much. Although . . ."

Anyone who didn't know Grey wouldn't have seen the subtle shake of his head. I caught it.

"Although?" Dumbo Cop prodded.

"She didn't like her ex-husband." His pen stopped moving for a moment, then he resumed scribbling without looking up. Heck, at this point he could be doodling a picture of Mickey Mouse for all I knew.

"Did you hear anyone threaten Ms. Michaels?" he asked.

"The smaller list is who hasn't threatened Mona."

"Which list are you on?" He finally looked at me.

I glanced at Grey for direction.

"Why stop now?" he sighed.

"It's all over town. You'll find out sooner or later. I didn't threaten to kill her, but I did have a public argument with her at the Fur Ball. And then again today at my boutique."

"You argued today? About what?"

"She wanted me to make a public apology for what happened at the Fur Ball."

"What happened?"

I could feel my face warm. "I spilled my wine, and some may have got on her dress."

His eyebrows rose, and his lips twitched. "I see."

"I had nothing to do with her death. I can account for my whereabouts all day."

"Let's start with where you were this morning."

As the police took my statement, with Grey at my side silently leading me along, Detective Judd Malone walked through the front door. He could never do undercover work. He exuded the Miranda Rights by simply breathing. His uniform consisted of jeans, blue shirt and black leather jacket.

He'd recognize Caro's name. He was pretty much annoyed by the fact that they shared the same air, let alone that she had poked her nose in his murder investigation.

"Detective Malone," I whispered.

Everyone turned in his direction.

The uniformed officers stood a little taller. Malone's gaze traveled between all of us and rested on Grey and me. Unlike the other two, Malone had the neutral gaze down. There was no question who was in charge. I seriously doubted he'd be snookered by a handshake. Even

Grey's.

Once Malone intersected our circle, the uniformed duo fell all over themselves to update him. Apparently, the other two officers had found Mona and Fluffy and had "secured the crime scene."

I was about to introduce myself when Grey squeezed my hand.

"Detective Malone. Grey Donovan. This is my fiancée, Melinda Langston. She found the victim."

Malone's unreadable expression gave nothing away except he was making mental notes of some kind. "I need to ask you some questions. Wait here."

He didn't kill time waiting for a response; he just left us standing there, assuming we'd obey. I could see why Caro found him obnoxious.

He was back within a few minutes. He had a brief conversion with the cops who had questioned me, then he made his way over to us.

I told him what I knew, and he scribbled in his notebook. He seemed satisfied, but it was hard to tell. He informed me he'd check my alibi and handed me his business card—in case I remembered something important later. Like what, I had no idea.

And the word "alibi" made me a tad nervous.

I kept my relationship with Caro to myself. If he didn't know we were cousins, I wasn't about to bring it up.

"What about Fluffy?" I asked.

Malone looked up from his little black notebook. "What about her?"

"Where are you taking her?"

He shrugged a broad shoulder. "To the ARL."

I shook my head. Wasn't he listening to me? I had just explained why that wasn't an option. "They won't take her. Call if you want, but you're wasting your time. Trust me, Don Furry was adamant. There's no room."

I felt a twinge of pity for Don as I realized he wasn't going to get his big contribution after all. Maybe they'd get lucky and Mona had named the ARL in her will.

Detective Malone didn't look too thrilled to be ambushed by my objections. "Don't move." He walked away and pulled out his cell phone.

It had taken him a while, maybe thirty minutes, but when he came back he gave me the once over again. The hair on the back of my neck stood at attention. I had a bad feeling. Had he called Don? Surely he confirmed he'd stopped by the boutique.

"Your cousin says you'll take Fluffy," he said.

"What?" I sputtered.

He'd obviously known who I was. I could understand why he'd kept that to himself, but why on God's green earth would Caro throw me under the bus? "I don't want her."

Malone looked bored. "I was able to confirm Don Furry was at Bow Wow. As you said, they're full. That dog would never survive the pound. It's you or nothing."

"It's just for tonight, Mel," Grey said. He gave me that look I hated. I imagined it was the same one he gave a suspect as he worked them into a confession. I narrowed my eyes and gave it right back.

The missing police officers came trotting down the staircase. "That dog needs drugs. She's mean."

Against my will, the image of Mona sprawled on the floor and Fluffy laying beside her popped into my head.

"She's not mean. She's protecting her human." I pointed at Malone. "Tonight only. Tomorrow she goes to the ARL." I broke away from the Good Ole' Boys Club and rushed up the stairs, with an audience trailing right behind.

"You can't go up there," someone yelled.

"I've already been up here." I pointed out the obvious.

I stopped at the doorway to Fluffy's room. She was exactly where I'd left her, next to Mona. My heart broke.

She was a dog. How was she ever going to understand she had to bond with someone new?

"This place is a disaster," Grey said softly.

"Probably a robbery interrupted," someone muttered.

"Cliff." I spun around and bumped into Dumbo Cop.

"Who?" the uniforms asked in unison.

"Mona's ex. Cliff." I looked past all the police and focused on Grey. "Someone needs to call him. I bet he'll take Fluffy." I couldn't keep the excited desperation out of my voice.

Cliff, the reason I was here in the first place, was suddenly the answer to the dog situation.

"Mona wouldn't want him to take her dog," Grey said.

"Legally, Fluffy is half his," I argued.

"Do you have his number?" Detective Malone asked.

"Not on me. It's at my shop." I refused to feel guilty. If Mona hadn't gone and gotten herself killed, Fluffy wouldn't have to go to Cliff's.

Fluffy got up and slowly walked across the room, leaving a trail of dark red paw prints on the hardwood floor. She stood in front of me and nuzzled my hand.

"Melinda. She chooses you." Grey's voice wrapped around me and squeezed the part of my heart I'd worked so hard to keep protected.

I didn't want to deal with this anymore. I didn't want to do the right thing. I didn't want to be chosen.

Fluffy rested her head in the palm of my hand, her dark eyes speaking thoughts I didn't understand. There was that dog language thing again.

I knew, *I knew*, I'd regret what I was about to do the moment I spoke the words. I pushed out a resigned sigh.

I was taking home a dog I didn't really like to a dog I loved.

I whirled around, hands on hips, eyes narrowed. Defenses and attitude back in place. "For one night only. Got it? Tomorrow she goes home with Cliff."

"Fine," Malone agreed.

Thinking back on it, he didn't really agree it was just for one night.

"It's going to be okay." I patted Fluffy's head and stroked the few non-sticky parts I could find.

"Oh, girl, there is no way you're getting into my Jeep covered in blood. We've got to call Armando. You need some TLC."

I looked up and caught my reflection in the antique mirror across the room.

"Holy cow, we both need some TLC."

Chapter Eight

Malone was more than a little touchy about the number of civilians who'd already tromped through his crime scene. I patiently explained, for the third time, Armando was the only stylist allowed to touch Mona's dog.

"I don't give a rat's ass about *Almando*. You're not poking around potential evidence."

I snickered because I knew he'd gotten the name wrong on purpose. Hanging out with the guy for the last hour, I'd realized he was a lot like Grey.

"You can stand guard. Make sure I don't touch anything. I only need his phone number."

"I can arrest you instead." There was no doubt in his tone. I had crossed the line.

Yup, he was a lot like Grey. Except Grey loved me and overlooked my flaws. Malone, on the other hand, had zero patience for me.

We were at a stubborn impasse. Unfortunately, he had the law on his side. I turned my back on Malone and dug out my cell from the bottom of my black Alexander Wang tote.

I had waited for an hour while Fluffy was "processed" before she was officially released into my care. She wasn't getting into my Jeep without a shampoo, blow out and a trim to even out the chunk of hair the police had snipped for evidence.

If I couldn't have Armando, I'd take Jade, the senior stylist at Divine Dog Spa. Everyone, human and animal, loved her. She was presumptuous, bold and one of those rare stylists who actually had great hair. To top it all off, she possessed the most endearing British accent.

It was that adorable accent that disguised her acid tongue. Most people were so enraptured with the tone of her voice they didn't pay attention to the meaning of her words. It could be minutes, or days, until you realized she'd just verbally spanked you *and* your dog.

I had Jade's number in my contacts and quickly reached her.

"I need your help." I gave the *Cliffs Notes* version of the current events.

"Mona's dead?" she squeaked.

I caught my breath as the reality of the situation hit me again. "Yes."

"I just love a good scandal. I'll be there in fifteen minutes."

Her excessive willingness to help wasn't about her concern for Mona. It was all about getting her hands on Fluffy. And morbid curiosity.

"I'll tell the security guard—"

Malone walked in front of me and cut me off. "Salinas," he shouted at the rookie cop guarding the front door. "If one more person shows up uninvited, arrest Ms. Langston on the spot."

I practically dropped the phone. "What?"

"Get off the phone, or I'll bag it as evidence."

Man, Mr. Personality he wasn't. "Fine. I get it. Jade, I'll have to bring Fluffy to you."

I ended the call and shoved my phone into the back pocket of my jeans, feeling somewhat reassured Malone wouldn't go digging around without a search warrant.

My back was up against the wall. There was no shampoo, no doggie conditioner, no detangler. And no professional on her way.

I'd be damned if I'd let Detective Malone get the best of me.

It seemed my best ideas came from the precipice of desperation. I hunted down Fluffy and coaxed her out of the house. I snapped on her leash and led her to the driveway.

That's how we ended up in Mona's fountain.

Girls Gone Wild, doggie style.

"I know this is your first time, but don't be afraid to splash a little." I led Fluffy slowly, giving her ample opportunity to roll around and become miraculously clean without having to touch her.

Her head hung, and her eyes lacked her typical sparkle. She wasn't a dog gone wild type. No splashing. No chomping water. She was nothing like Missy, who'd be prancing and eating water as if it were goose pâté on a gourmet dog biscuit.

Truth be told, Fluffy looked a touch embarrassed to be bathing where all the neighbors could see her. And another thing—once wet, she resembled a skinny greyhound.

"Hey Salinas," I yelled out, "can you ask Malone for a towel?" I looked at my soaked jeans. "Make that two. Oh, and Fluffy's hair brush."

He shook his bulbous bald head. "The house is a crime scene."

I was seriously going to yell the next time someone spoke the words "crime scene."

"I think it's obvious what killed Mona, and it wasn't a dog brush or a couple of towels."

Officer Salinas puffed out his chest and crossed his arms. "There may have been a robbery. We have to account for everything. I can't do it."

Of course he couldn't. Cops were such pansy rule followers.

I looked over at Grey who was leaning against his favorite toy, his brand new Mercedes SUV. I was disappointed he'd opted out of the Roadster. Grey said he needed something to transport his "art" more than he needed speed. I suggested he get both; he could afford it. He rejected that idea as "too extravagant."

We lived in Orange County. "Extravagant" was our zip code.

Fluffy shook, sending streams of water everywhere. My anxiety level was at its max. *Breathe in. Breathe out.*

Grey watched me squeeze water from my t-shirt while he talked on his cell phone. At some point he'd slipped off his suit jacket and had rolled his shirt sleeves to his elbows.

"Grey," I called out, pointing at Fluffy who looked like a giant wet rat.

He nodded and wrapped up his call, then moved to the back of his car and popped the trunk.

He pulled out a beach blanket and brought it over, covering Fluffy. "I always imagined she was bigger under all that hair."

Fluffy shivered for a few seconds as she burrowed into the soft flannel material. My heart broke for Grey when I realized the blanket was Colbalt's, Grey's foster Weimaraner.

Last month, the Weimaraner rescue agency in LA had found a permanent home for Colbie. Grey had been heartbroken. Both Caro and I had warned him he'd ultimately want to keep the dog, but Grey hadn't heeded our advice. This was one instance I wish I'd been wrong.

"Who were you talking to?" I asked as I rubbed down Fluffy.

"It's not important."

Code for, I can't tell you.

"Can you believe Malone wouldn't cough up a measly towel?" I asked, willing to change the subject.

"Heartless," he deadpanned.

"Did you see that painting in Mona's room? The one above her bed?"

He nodded. "Thomas Cole. She has, had, a lot of valuable art."

"If you find something by Cole, I want one."

"He's not cheap." He changed the subject. "Now what?"

I looked at Fluffy—dejected and wet—cocooned in a red plaid blanket. I sighed, thinking of everything I needed to do. "I've got to get home to Missy. I called Darby and asked her to stop by the house, but I got her voicemail."

"I can pick up Missy."

"Thanks. Because of Malone, we've got you-know-who to account for also." I nodded toward Mona's pride and joy. "Fluffy's not so fluffy anymore. Jade offered to make a house call but Malone nixed that idea."

"I'm sure he did. Drop off Fluffy. While they fix her, we'll grab a bite from Gina's."

My stomach growled thinking about my favorite pizza—pepperoni, meatballs, Italian sausage, and bacon. "The Godfather and Ricotta sticks."

Grey grabbed my shoulders and kissed me hard on the lips. "It's a date. I'm glad you called."

I shrugged, surprised at the sincerity in his voice. "Who else would I call?"

"With you, I never know." Grey climbed into his SUV and drove off.

I loaded Fluffy and myself into the Jeep. I grabbed a snood from the glove box and pulled it over her head, but it was little protection. I tightened the blanket around her and fastened it with an old plastic hair clip I'd found with the hood.

I called Jade and gave her a heads up that we were on our way. I shot a sideways glance at Her Highness. Her hair was going to be tangled beyond repair. If Jade was smart, she'd call in reinforcements.

As we weaved our way out of the neighborhood, I noticed that other than the police vehicles the streets were empty. It was unusual for this time of evening. I swear I caught a few nosey bodies peeking out their mansion windows with binoculars.

I rolled to a stop at the security gate. The guard who'd waved me in earlier was still manning his station.

"I'm sure you've heard about Mona by now," I said, squeezing the steering wheel. I wasn't sure what to say.

He nodded.

"I've got Fluffy for the night." I motioned in her direction.

He looked around me. His unibrow rose when he saw Fluffy's sad hound dog expression on her regal face.

He pushed up his bifocals. "Ms. Michaels would appreciate knowing her Fluffy is with someone who cares so much."

I wrinkled my nose. I wouldn't go so far as to categorize myself as someone who cared, but I wasn't about to argue with him. His eyes were red rimmed, like he'd been crying. No need to add to his distress.

"I'm sure we'll see each other again." I waved good-bye and drove off. I glanced in my review mirror and watched as he pulled his cap over his face.

He had to be the only person in town who'd shed a tear for Mona Michaels.

That's when I thought about Tricia.

I didn't envy the person who had to tell her that her best friend was not only dead, but murdered.

Chapter Nine

The second I pulled up to the Divine Spa, Jade flew out the front door in her four-inch Christian Louboutin heels and black Gucci pantsuit.

"I was absolutely gobsmacked to hear about Mona. Tell me everything." Jade clapped her hands together as if summoning Tinkerbelle, which seemed fitting since they had the same hair.

I hopped out of the Jeep, my boots slapping the asphalt. "There's not much to tell."

Jade shot me an impatient look. "How did she die?"

I didn't answer right away, measuring my words. I made my way to the passenger side. I flung the door open and unharnessed Fluffy. "Someone hit her in the head . . . with Fluffy's Emmy."

Jade peered over my shoulder and gasped. "Bloody hell. She looks beastly."

"I told you she needed a lot of work."

"Is she wearing a burka?"

I removed the hair clip and tugged off the blanket. Fluffy shivered. I clipped the leash on Fluffy's collar, and she gingerly jumped on to the sidewalk in one effortless motion. She stood tall and erect, the tip of her tail poised like a telescope. Her version of I-don't-need-you.

Think again, girl. She looked like she'd rolled in a back alley Dumpster.

Jade pushed the snood off Fluffy's head. "Why is she wet? Are you a suspect?"

"I wasn't allowed to use the tub so I took her for a walk in the fountain. No, I'm not a suspect." Although, Malone hadn't actually spoken those words out loud. Well, shoot.

"The fountain in the driveway?" Her blond eyebrows disappeared behind her bangs. "You did have a row with Mona not that long ago."

"So?"

"You tossed her and Tricia out of Bow Wow."

"That doesn't mean I killed her."

"Did you brush her?"

Good grief, it was difficult keeping up with her ping-pong conversation. Hopefully she was talking about Fluffy. "No."

"Good. You don't have the proper tools and could have damaged the coat."

I dragged a hand through my hair and rubbed my head. I had no idea what she was talking about. I owned a bulldog. There wasn't much to brush. Wet or dry.

She grabbed Fluffy's leash from my grip. "I always thought Mona was barking mad. Any real suspects?"

"Look, I doubt Malone wants people speculating about what happened. So, if you can keep this to yourself . . ." I trailed off hoping she'd understand. Malone hadn't ordered me to keep my mouth shut, but I couldn't imagine him happy about people gossiping about his case.

"Absolutely." Jade stroked Fluffy's head compassionately. "This is going to take much longer than I anticipated. I'll phone you in a few hours."

"I'll be at Gina's." I took one last look at Fluffy and tried to imagine what Mona would say if she could see her dog now.

With a nod, Jade was off. "Okay, My Lady. Come on in here and let's pamper you like you deserve." And then they disappeared into the salon.

Relieved I'd postponed my Fluffy responsibility at the eleventh-hour, I jumped in the Jeep and headed for Gina's. The cool night air raced against my face as I zoomed down PCH.

I spotted Grey sitting in the patio area, people watching. A huge goofy smile spread across my mouth. I whipped the Jeep around and quickly found a decent parking spot a block down the street from the restaurant.

I grabbed my tote and hustled toward my dates, practically falling onto the table as I reached them. Missy jumped around like a crazy dog, flinging drool on Grey's shoes. I crouched next to her and scratched behind her ears.

"Hi, girlfriend. How ya doing? Did you miss me?"

She licked my face and made silly snorting noises. I was overwhelmed with an unexpected sadness for Fluffy and her loss. My chest constricted. I hugged Missy tighter.

A jumble of conflicting emotions squeezed my heart as I looked up at Grey. "Thanks for getting her. I bet she was happy to see you."

Ever the gentleman, he pulled out my chair, then bent down and kissed my cheek. "Missy planted a few slobbery kisses to prove it."

I grabbed his face and planted a big fat kiss of my own on his lips. "Just the kind you like. You're the best."

"Only because I like your dog."

There was thirty pounds of truth in his off-handed remark. Missy jumped up on my leg, her pink tongue lapping the air. She was crazy, but she was *my* crazy dog.

"Sit down, Mel. Missy has no idea what's going on. The food will be ready any time."

"What?"

Grey regarded me with his intense green eyes. "She's picking up your stress."

Overwhelmed with exhaustion, I plopped onto the chair. Missy waddled back to Grey's side of the table and returned to her resting place. She stared at me, panting as if she'd just run a marathon. Grey was right. For Missy, the day was just like any other.

Alanis Morissette's version of "Crazy" sang out around us.

"You have a new ring tone." Grey took a drink of his bottled water.

I shook my head. "That's not mine."

"It's coming from your purse."

I reached into my tote, found my cell and held it up. "Not me."

My purse continued to sing . . . "*We're never gonna survive . . .*"

What the heck?

I rummaged around and found a second phone. I didn't recognize it at first, but I was familiar with the name on the screen. Tricia.

"Holy crapola." I had Mona's phone. I looked across the table at Grey, and I saw the question ready on his lips.

Without thinking about the consequences, I answered. "Hello? Hello…?"

Silence answered on the other end.

"Did they hang up?" Grey asked.

I nodded. "I guess so." I stared at the phone. How did I get Mona's cell? Then I remembered calling her shortly after arriving at her house.

Well heck, I could have called Armando at anytime. I thumbed through the contacts and found his unlisted number. I pulled out a receipt from my purse and jotted down his information.

"Whose phone?" Grey asked calmly.

My head snapped up like a guilty criminal. I opened my mouth to answer, when Uncle Sal (he wasn't really our uncle; that's what everyone called him) yelled out our number.

"Food's ready," I said.

Grey slowly pushed his chair back; his rugged face looked tired and slightly worried. Missy lumbered to the other side of the table and under my chair.

I'm not sure why he was concerned. I didn't steal the phone—I just accidently palmed it from Mona's house. I'd give it back. But I wanted to snoop first. Didn't everyone want to know who Mona had on speed dial?

I scrolled through Mona's contact list, seeing the names and numbers of people I expected: Teri Essman (the mayor), Tricia Edwards, Armando.

"Holy cow," I whispered. Darby Beckett's number was programmed as "ICE," In Case of Emergency. What was going on?

I looked around and saw Grey grabbing our food. I waved and blew him a kiss as my mind ran wild with questions. I leaned back, just out of his direct line of vision, then quickly did a little more snooping.

According to the phone history, Mona's last outgoing call was to Jo at 4:00 pm, and the last incoming call before mine was from Darby at 4:45 pm. That was when I had called Mona.

I looked up and saw Grey with our food. I fumbled with the phone as I turned it off and dropped it into my bag. My heart raced. He'd ask about the phone again.

I tapped my purse nervously. Grey wasn't a bend-the-rules-kinda-guy when it came to the law. He'd want me to turn the phone over to the police. Tonight. I didn't want to disappoint him, but Darby was my best friend, and I had her back.

I had to talk to Darby first. Once the police had Mona's cell, who knew what they'd think? Heck, *I* didn't know what to think.

Grey placed the food on the table and sat. My stomach growled. He pushed the appetizers in front of me. I grabbed a ricotta stick and took a bite.

"Who called?" he asked.

I looked down at my lap and brushed off a few crumbs. Oh, Lord. I didn't want to lie. I cleared my throat. "It wasn't for me."

"It's not your phone," he said.

I was at a complete loss for words and excuses. What's the saying? The silence was deafening.

"I don't want to tell you," I blurted, sweating like a turkey the day before Thanksgiving.

"I see." His face hardened. I could sense he was recalculating how to get the information he wanted.

By now my heart pounded so hard I was amazed Grey couldn't hear it. "Trust me," I said.

"If you're in some kind of trouble—"

"I'm not in trouble. I-I can't tell you right now. Honestly, it's not even that big of a deal."

"Then you shouldn't have a problem answering my question."

My nervousness started to grow into frustration. I dropped a slice of pizza onto my plate. "If you want 'us' to work, trust has to be a two-way street."

Grey leaned across the table, his eyes flashing a potluck of emotion. "I trust you with my life, and you know it. You're picking a fight for no reason."

"I'm not picking a fight."

"In my experience, when someone *purposely* hides the truth, it's always a big deal," Grey warned.

Warning noted and filed.

Chapter Ten

We'd survived Fluffy's overnight. Missy and I had shared a queen-sized bed with a king-sized Fluffy, and I'd dreamt about Grey's king-sized warning. By 9:00 am, I'd rolled out of bed a king-sized grump.

Once I'd walked the dogs (good grief; I didn't like picking up after such a big dog), I'd brushed my teeth, washed mine and Missy's faces, and pulled my hair back into a messy ponytail. Everything else would have to wait until after breakfast.

I shuffled around the sunshine-filled kitchen in my fuzzy bulldog slippers, Victoria's Secret sleeping shorts and tank top (yes, I'd walked the dogs in my PJ's; no one cares, trust me). I poured a bowl of my favorite cereal, Cap'n Crunch with Crunch Berries, then meandered out to the patio, leaving the French doors open so the dogs could join me.

I settled onto a wicker chair and propped up my feet. What I craved was a chai latte from the Koffee Klatch. If only they delivered. I closed my eyes, tipped my face to the sun and enjoyed the tranquility of the morning. I had a feeling I wasn't alone. I opened my eyes, and there stood Fluffy. She'd followed as far as the doorway.

"What?"

Fluffy looked back at Missy, who was in the kitchen chowing her scoop of food with one side of her mouth, while managing to drool out the other side at the same time. I'd have to clean the folds of Missy's face again after breakfast. If I didn't keep her clean and dry she'd develop dermatitis.

Fluffy returned her attention to me. I knew what she was communicating. Missy was noisy and messy. It was true. Bullies snorted, drooled and passed a lot of gas. But it was that imperfectness that I loved so dearly.

"Sorry, Your Highness, you'll have to deal with it."

Unimpressed, Fluffy backed up a couple of steps, then disappeared inside the house.

Once I'd finished my cereal, I shuffled back into the kitchen. I rinsed out my bowl and set it in the sink. I'd worry about the dishes later.

Or maybe I'd get lucky and Caro would "drop by." I *was* in possession of the brooch, which meant she was bound to show up eventually. I had a new hiding place for the pin. *Way* better than the cookie jar.

No one truly understood our competition over that Godawful heirloom. Not even Grey. But the brooch was all we had left of Grandma Tillie. She'd had this way of making us feel special, as if we were the only ones she really loved. It was possible that Grandma Tillie knew the brooch was the one thing that would keep Caro and me together.

Enough sappiness. I had more pressing issues. First things first, handing off Fluffy.

I'd lifted Cliff's number from Mona's phone last night. I headed to my bedroom and unplugged my cell from the charger. Bless her heart, Missy had followed me, snorting and shaking her head, leaving a trail of water and slobber on the hardwood floor.

I grabbed a hand towel from the master bath and quickly wiped up the slippery mess. I found a dry edge to blot the folds around her nose. Once she was clean, I tossed the towel onto the bathroom counter.

"Cross your fingers, girl." I punched in Cliff's number. Missy tilted her head, and we both waited as the phone rang and rang.

"Hello?"

I gave Missy the thumbs up. "Hey Cliff, it's Melinda. Melinda Langston. I—" It suddenly dawned on me he might not know about Mona. "Uh, I just wondered if you'd heard about Mona?"

"Yeah. The police called last night." He mumbled like he had a mouthful of rocks. Or I'd woken him up from a drunken stupor.

"I'm sorry," I said.

"The well's officially run dry. Not that I've seen a single penny in the past month."

Fluffy suddenly appeared in the hallway. I frowned at her as she shimmied her way in between Missy and me.

"Mona paid you support?" That was news to me.

"It was a private matter."

I could hear the clinking of ice against glass and then a slurp. You know, that slurp men thought was appropriate when they drank Scotch. I'm no prude, but 10:00 am was a little early to be drinking.

"I had no idea," I said.

"That's why it's called private," he ground out.

Good grief, he could compete with Mona for Jerk of the Year.

Missy slipped beneath the bed looking for a cool spot to take a nap.

Fluffy sprawled out at the foot of the bed, watching me with her intense eyes. I turned my back on her and cleared my throat. "Well, the reason I called was to arrange a pick-up time."

"For what?"

"Fluffy."

His dark manic laughter burst into my ear. "She's as big of a pain in my ass as my ex. Unless it's cash, Scotch or a trip to Vegas, you don't have anything I want."

I walked into the bathroom and closed the door, feeling the need for privacy. "But you have joint custody."

"I only fought for custody so I wouldn't have to pay Mona dog support. It bugged the hell out of Mona that I had her precious Fluffy."

That rumor was true. What a cad. "But you're supposed to take her every Wednesday."

"I was. Now she's yours."

"No." I shook my head. "Fluffy is not my responsibility." I did not have the patience to take care of a high maintenance dog.

"Possession is nine-tenths of the law," he said. "If she doesn't get her afternoon snack, she's a real pisser. Good luck."

The line went dead.

As Grandma Tillie used to say, "He makes a hornet look cuddly." No wonder Mona kicked his butt to the curb.

I opened the door a crack and peeked into the bedroom. Missy had come out from under the bed and was now lying alongside Fluffy, staring at me as if I'd lost my mind hiding in the bathroom. I closed the door so I could think without being stared at.

Now what?

Chapter Eleven

Fluffy was like an unexpected pimple the day of an eveningwear competition. As ugly and as painful as it may be, neither the pimple nor Fluffy were going anywhere soon. Fluffy wasn't a bad dog. It was me; I'm a one-dog woman.

After quick shower, I threw on a pair of sand-colored cargo pants, a purple tank top, a hoodie and my flip flops. The dogs and I hopped in the Jeep and took a chance we'd find Darby at Paw Prints. It was time for a chat.

We were in luck. The "Open" sign hung in the door of the studio. I pulled into the empty parking spot behind the FedEx truck, which had selfishly staked out two spaces.

The three of us enthusiastically tumbled out of the Jeep, and the dogs instantly made a beeline for Bow Wow.

"Not today, guys. We're here to see Darby."

Missy twirled in a half circle, changing directions. Fluffy on the other hand, fixed her eyes on the Bow Wow door and barreled her way past me and toward her target.

I stopped so abruptly my purse slid down my arm and hung on the leash, halting Fluffy in her stubborn tracks. I swore under my breath.

"Listen. We have got to come to an agreement," I demanded.

Her Highness turned in my direction. A wisp of fur fell into her eyes. She flipped it back with the shake of her head. Doggie language for "I'm not listening to you."

"Google alert, Fluffy. It's not all about you anymore." By the time my dog-sitting stint was over, I'd have an ulcer.

Missy sat on the sidewalk, her tongue hanging out. If she could talk I'm sure she'd want to know why we were just standing there. My little Miss Congeniality. I loved her more than an A-list celeb loved their Hermes Birkin bag.

"Let's go." I headed toward Paw Prints, and the dogs followed—one happy-go-lucky, the other as pretentious as a bed-hopping politician.

We strolled inside the studio. "Guess who?" I called out.

Paw Prints was as unique as its owner. The studio was an unfinished high-end warehouse. Except for the lobby. It was straight out of the Victorian era, including a silver antique tea set on a side table.

The working portion of the studio was wide open with a variety of adorable and goofy pet portraits hanging on the walls, props stored on metal shelves, and a handful of lights and umbrellas.

Darby, in her bohemian wrap skirt and white, lacy sleeveless top, dragged a second Adirondack chair to her staging area.

"Hi," she said as she turned around. Her white beret slipped off her head. She caught it one-handed. "Ah, you have Fluffy."

"It's my curse." I unhooked the dogs and dropped the leashes on the front desk.

Missy bumbled over to the box of toys Darby kept for her clients. She rummaged around and pulled out a rubber chicken and immediately demonstrated she was the alpha dog.

Fluffy, on the other hand, sniffed the velvet covered couches in the lobby, not entirely sure of where I'd taken her, and if she was staying.

"I thought you dropped her off last night." Darby pulled down a swimming pool backdrop, which set off her scene perfectly. All it needed was a couple of umbrella drinks.

"I tried."

"So she stayed with you?" Darby asked, with a small disbelieving chuckle.

"Yeah." I fumbled for what to say next. "Who's coming?" I pointed toward her set-up, eager to change the subject while I searched for the right way to break the news about Mona.

"Mandy Beenerman's bringing in her Lhasa Apso."

I shook my head. "I can't place her, but her name sounds really familiar."

"She owns the fitness company, Mandy's Place." Darby continued to arrange and rearrange props as she talked. "Apparently Nietzsche has agoraphobia. Since your cousin has taken them on as clients, he's gotten better, and this is his reward."

"You've talked to Caro?"

Darby stood back and studied her masterpiece. "No. Mandy. But Caro did recommend me. I need to call and thank her. Unless you want to?" She grinned at me over her shoulder.

"You're such a comedian."

"So what's going on?" she asked.

I walked over to one of the chairs she'd just positioned to picture perfection and sat, dropping my purse between my feet. "I'm taking the day off."

She swiveled in my direction. "Why?"

Sometimes the direct approach was best. "Mona's dead."

Eyes wide open, Darby looked horrified. "What do you mean, dead?"

"Like someone whacked with her Fluffy's Emmy. Gone. Dead."

She tripped over the light stand making her way to me. "She's been murdered? Are you sure?"

"Trust me, she's dead. I've seen her." I shuddered, remembering Mona's awkward pose.

Darby shook her head, obviously confused. "When?" her voice cracked. I watched her normally effortless smile slip away.

"Last night. I took Fluffy home, and she found her," I continued, "Mona was lying on the floor with the Emmy . . ." I pointed to my head.

Darby looked around the studio and zeroed in on Mona's dog, sprawled out on the cowhide rug on the far side of the studio.

"That's awful."

"I certainly could have gone my entire lifetime without seeing it."

Darby suddenly jumped up and nervously repositioned the lighting. "Do the police know who did it?" Her tone suggested it was an afterthought, but her sideways glance cast a hint of guilt for even being curious. It must be those midwestern manners that kept her from admitting she wanted more details.

"The police mentioned it may have been a robbery gone wrong. That she might have interrupted someone ransacking Fluffy's room."

She picked up her camera and thoroughly checked it out. "You saw her. Is that what you think?"

Missy trotted over with her rubber chicken, her nails clicking on the cement floor. She dropped the toy in front of me for a game a fetch. "It's possible. The room was a mess."

I tossed the chicken to where Fluffy was napping. Missy chased after it, slipping on a throw rug.

"What about Jo's dream?" Darby asked matter-of-factly, snapping pictures of Missy's antics.

I rolled my eyes, thinking about psychic Jo. "She *said* she had a dream."

She lowered the camera and looked at me. "You don't believe her?"

"No, I don't believe for one minute Fluffy came to her in a dream to warn her about something. Do you?"

Darby shrugged. "I don't know." She checked her watch. "I don't mean to rush you, but Mandy will be here anytime." She clipped the camera back onto the tripod.

I stood up and slung my bag onto my shoulder. "I just thought you'd want to know what had happened."

"I appreciate it," she answered softly.

I waited until she faced me, then said, "I tried to call you last night."

"Oh?"

"Around four-thirty. And then again two or three times after that. I left you messages. Why haven't you called me back?"

She finger combed her curls until they sprung apart. "I-I must have been running errands and didn't hear it . . . or maybe . . . I left it here," she explained slowly as if she was making it up as she went along.

"Are you saying you lost your phone?"

"I haven't needed it. I just assumed it was in my bag. I don't charge it every night."

I walked over to Darby, my best friend, so she had to look me in the eye. "You didn't call Mona yesterday?"

She chewed her lower lip, eyebrows askew. "What?"

"There was a missed call on Mona's phone. It was your number."

She fingered the gold heart charm around her neck. "Maybe it only looked like my number."

I pulled Mona's phone from my purse. "No, I'm pretty sure it's yours. She's got your name programmed into her contacts—"

Darby reached for the phone. "Oh, my gosh. Where'd you get that?"

I pulled my hand away. "It was on her hallway table in the foyer."

"Why is it in your purse?"

"I picked it up by accident. Stop changing the subject. Why did you call Mona?"

"I-I . . . " Darby's cheeks flushed, and she seemed to change her mind about what she was going to say. "I thought Cliff left Fluffy without a leash, so I called to tell her to bring one," her voice rose.

My stomach turned, knowing she was lying. I had Fluffy's lead, and we both knew it.

"Darby, is there something going on I don't know about?"

"No. What about you? You kicked Mona out of Bow Wow, after you tossed wine on her dress. You have to get rid of that." She waved toward the phone. "Once the police find out about . . .your confrontations, they're going to question you."

I sighed at her accurate summarization. "They already know. I'm taking the phone to Detective Malone, but I wanted to talk to you first."

She struggled as if wanting to ask me a question but not sure how. Or maybe she wasn't sure if she should say anything. Either way, she stood frozen, staring at me like a mime with stage fright.

"What? What's going on inside your head?"

"You're going to take Mona's phone to the police?"

"I have to. Unless you can give me a really good reason why not."

She shook her head. "No. You have to hand it over."

We stood in silence for a few minutes, both lost in our own thoughts. Missy brought back the chicken for another throw.

"They're going to ask you about that call," I said softly. "Do you want to talk about it?"

She waved away my concern with a shaky hand. "It's not important. I didn't even ask if you're okay. I'm sure finding Mona was . . . disturbing."

"I've definitely seen my fill of dead bodies. Once I turn over the phone, the police are going to want to know why you're programmed as an emergency contact."

"I swear, I don't know. It doesn't make any sense. She made it perfectly clear she didn't like me." She looked away.

"Darb, it wasn't personal. I don't think she liked anyone or anything other than Fluffy. If you don't know, you don't know. Good grief, don't go and make something up. We can't always answer for other people's actions."

She looked at me, an emotion I couldn't decipher swirling in her eyes. "Mona didn't care who she hurt." There was a hint of what sounded like betrayal in her voice.

"You're right." I called the dogs. Missy immediately dropped the chicken she'd been slobbering over and trotted towards us. Fluffy didn't twitch. I rubbed Missy's head affectionately then clipped on her leash. "Grey knows I have someone's phone, he just doesn't realize it belongs to Mona."

"Is that bad?"

"Not for you."

Darby sighed. "Mel, don't lie to Grey because of me."

I hugged my best friend. "I didn't lie. Do me a favor. Take some time to get all your facts straight. If you need a lawyer, call Grey. He'll refer you to someone."

She flinched under my embrace. "You think I need a lawyer?" she squeaked and pulled away. "I thought you said the police thought it was a robbery."

"Think about it. In less than a week, Jo, Cliff, Tova, you, and I have all had some type of altercation with Mona. At some point, the police are going to want to talk to you."

"I guess so."

I called Fluffy again, and she continued to ignore me. Darby and I stared at the giant fluff ball sprawled on her back, feet in the air, wiggling side to side.

"She's going to have a bad case of bed-head when she gets up," Darby said.

"Great. I guess we're going to see Jade again."

"Again?"

I marched over to Fluffy. She scrambled to her feet and shook. Stray hair flew everywhere. "Trust me, you don't want to know. Maybe I could just leave her with you?"

"She doesn't like me any more than Mona did." Darby checked her watch again. "Mandy's late."

I attached Fluffy's leash, then grabbed the lead Missy had dragged across the floor when she followed me. "All right, dogs, Darby's kicking us out of here for a paying gig."

Darby looked sad. I wasn't expecting her to feel so badly about Mona. "It's going to be fine." I tried to sound reassuring.

"I know." She didn't look convinced.

She was hiding something, and I had a feeling it was going to be a doozie when it came out.

Secrets never stay secret. I'd learned that the hard way.

Sure as shootin', Darby Beckett had her own secrets.

Chapter Twelve

I felt like a total dog, and I knew a lot about dogs. I believed Darby didn't know Mona had listed her as an emergency contact. But she had flat out lied about why she'd called Mona. And for the life of me, I couldn't figure out why.

I called the police station to make sure Malone was in. He was out for the day. So the dogs and I stopped at the Bark Park, Laguna's dog park—two acres of fenced-in grass and very popular with both dogs and humans.

Our odd trio stepped through the first gate easily enough. I unleashed Fluffy, then opened the second gate. She sat perfectly erect, waiting for someone to direct her movements.

"Run. Go play. Be free." I motioned to the wide open space where a pack of dogs ran at top speed. She remained frozen, looking at me for the right command. Wow. The Bark Park was total culture shock for a pampered pooch.

Missy continued to sit patiently at my feet. "Okay, Fluffy, Missy here will show you how it's done."

I unclipped the leash, and Missy was off like a shot. Spin, spin, spin. Jump, jump, jump. Pause and breathe. And then off to chase an invisible object a good fifty yards before she collapsed in a heap of dog under the trees. It was always the same.

"See how much fun you can have? Go on, run around like Missy."

Fluffy watched me for a full ten seconds before she stood and gingerly walked through the second gate and into the actual park.

She looked back at me, and I waved at her as I closed the gate behind us. "Go on. You're fine." Sheesh.

Once Fluffy decided to let her hair down and act like a dog, she ran as if she'd been held captive for the first half of her life.

Hop, hop, run. A cut to the left. Then a cut to the right. She abruptly burst into a gallop, her silky hair blew back from her face, and her pink tongue hung out of her mouth (not that she'd ever admit to doing something so dog-like as to have her tongue exposed in an undignified manner). I had to admit, she was beautiful to watch.

I grabbed the collapsible dog bowls I'd brought and filled them with water. At some point the "kids" would be thirsty. As soon as Missy saw what I was doing, she was at my feet chugging, slurping and dripping water everywhere. And sneezing. Grass allergies.

I threw her the disc for a while, then she was back at the water bowl. Once she'd had her fill, we camped out on a park bench (I sat on the bench, Missy, who was worn out, sprawled out underneath) and let Fluffy run. I worried if I interacted with her, she'd return to her pent-up snob-dog ways.

It wasn't long before a couple of black and tan Salukis joined her. The three of them raced around playing their version of tag, Fluffy losing. Out of nowhere, Fluffy made a sharp cut to the right and whipped around. Suddenly, she was chasing them. Her agility was amazing.

The Salukis' owner, a tall, blond, twenty-something decked out in skinny jeans and an oversized Gap sweatshirt, warily watched Missy and me from the opposite end of the bench. Who knows why she found us so fascinating, but she was definitely staring at us.

I scrutinized her from behind my sunglasses.

While we waited for Fluffy to tire, I dug out my cell and called Jade for advice on brushing an Afghan. She recited a monologue of products I "needed" in order to keep Fluffy in mint condition.

That dog used more hair product than Miss Texas.

Jade's list went in one ear and out the other. I wasn't going to have Fluffy long enough to invest in that amount of grooming supplies. I just wanted to know if I could use the brush I'd bought for Missy but hadn't ever used.

The short answer was no.

Jade promised if we stopped by the spa she'd have the correct grooming tools waiting for me with some dude named Kendall. I was certain Mona owned all those brushes, combs, barrettes and whatever else Jade yammered on about. Honestly, it wasn't really going to hurt anything if Fluffy went one whole day without proper brushing.

I politely passed, and she arrogantly warned I'd be sorry in her British accent that somehow made her verbal abuse acceptable.

"Isn't that Mona Michaels' dog?" The Salukis' owner had finally gathered her courage to ask her burning question.

"Yes." I tucked my cell into my bag and braced myself for the inquisition about Mona's death and why I had Fluffy.

She continued to stare.

What? Did I have something stuck between my teeth? Maybe she was checking out her reflection in my lenses.

"How fast do you think they're running?" I asked, turning our focus to the dogs.

"I've clocked them at thirty-eight miles an hour."

My head snapped in her direction. "Seriously?"

She nodded. "Affies love to run. Definitely keep her on the leash if you're not in an enclosed area. Are you the new dog walker?"

Affies? I smiled thinking about how insulted Fluffy would be to know she'd been reduced to a common nickname. A giggle tickled the back of my throat, but I managed to keep it back.

She continued to look at me funny. I realized she'd asked a question.

"No," I said.

She narrowed her eyes. "Are you family?"

"More of a family friend." I cringed even as I said it. She was entirely too interested in Mona and Fluffy. It was possible someone had blabbed to the media about Mona's death. "Do you know Mona?"

"I'm Fluffy's dog walker."

Oh. "Well, this is awkward, isn't it?"

"If I haven't been replaced, who are you really?"

I wasn't sure what to say, so I went with the truth. "My mother and Mona really are childhood friends. I'm temporarily dog-sitting."

She didn't look like she believed me.

"Do you walk her every day?" This was the first I'd heard about a dog walker. Where had Blondie been hiding?

"A couple of times a week. I care for a number of dogs in her community."

"I see."

"You're not Cliff's girlfriend?" she asked.

"Heck, no. Why would you even think that? Have you met Cliff?"

"He seems like the kind of guy who'd throw a younger woman in his ex's face." The edgy tone implied she wasn't a member of Team Cliff.

"Oh?"

She shrugged as if downplaying what she was about to say. "He stopped by last week, and they had an argument."

"About?"

"I couldn't tell, but neither one of them were happy. There was a lot of yelling."

"Was that Wednesday?"

"No. Sunday afternoon."

The day of the Fur Ball.

I lowered my sunglasses and turned toward her. "I didn't catch your name."

"Kate."

I held out my hand. "I'm Melinda. My friends call me Mel."

"I'm glad you stopped by the park today. There aren't many dogs who can keep up with Crash and Lou Lou."

Kate seemed like a nice person, and I felt a tad dishonest not telling her about Mona. I grabbed Missy's leash and clipped it to her collar. "I think Fluffy enjoyed herself. It was nice chatting with you, but we've got to go. Fluffy. Come," I called.

She took one look at me and ran the opposite direction. I hadn't thought this part through very well. I called her again. She continued to ignore me.

Kate let out an ear-piercing whistle and her dogs immediately came running, Fluffy bringing up the rear.

"Thanks." I grabbed Fluffy while I had the chance. I attached her lead, regaining control of the situation.

"Remember, I'm the human." That was becoming a frequent reprimand.

"You might want to suggest to Mona obedience training. I don't know if you've heard of her, but Carolina Lamont's the best here in town. She's a pet behaviorist."

I groaned inwardly. "I've heard of her."

Too bad my cousin couldn't have helped Mona with *her* behavioral issues. Maybe she'd still be alive today. And in possession of her precious Fluffy.

I'd just loaded the dogs into the Jeep when my cell phone rang.

"Everybody hold tight." I frantically searched my bag. "Geesh. Hold on," I yelled as it rang. My fingers found my phone at the bottom of my bag. Unknown caller. Hmm. Odds were it was a telemarketer. Or my mama. It would be just like her to call from an unlisted number so I'd pick up.

"What do you think, Missy? Should I answer it?"

It was Missy's turn to ride shotgun. She sneezed, then shook her head, beating herself with her jowls. I wiped her slimy drool off my leg and answered the phone.

"Hello?"

"Melinda Sue Langston?"

I squinted at Missy. I'd been had. "Depends. Who's calling?"

"Owen Quinn, Mona Michael's attorney," a high pitched male voice spoke quickly.

"Uh. Yes, this is Melinda." I couldn't stop myself from looking in the rearview mirror at the backseat. "Are you calling about Fluffy?"

Hearing her name she looked in my direction. Her eyes fixated on my reflection.

"I need you to stop by my office tomorrow," he said.

"Why?"

"I'd-prefer-to explain-in-person-would-11:00-am-work-for-you?"

Good grief, he talked fast. I brushed a few stray hairs away from my face. "Where are you located?"

He rattled off an address downtown, not far from Bow Wow.

"Do I need to bring anything? Like a dog?" I eyeballed Fluffy over the top of my sunglasses.

"That's not necessary. I'll see you then, Ms. Langston."

He disconnected, and I was left wondering what his call was really about. Great. Now what?

Grey called late that night. I had every intention of explaining about Mona's phone and Owen Quinn, the man with two first names. Until Grey said he was leaving town on an art forgery case.

I tossed my boots into the walk-in closet with more effort than needed. "When?"

"I'm taking a red-eye out of LAX tonight."

I knew better than to ask where he was going. I closed my eyes and inhaled deeply. I could hear flight departure announcements over the phone. He was already at the airport. "How long?"

"I don't know. A couple of days. It'll depend on the validity of the lead."

I ignored the apprehension twisting in my stomach. He promised to call when he landed. I promised to stay out of trouble.

Since I didn't have a date with Grey, I slipped on my PJ's and had a date with the TV.

"Stay off the couch," I said to Fluffy.

She dismissed my order with a shrug and promptly climbed up on my leather couch and made herself at home.

"Down." I pointed to the floor next to Missy who was curled into a tight ball in her doggie bed, drooling in her sleep.

Fluffy closed her eyes and drifted off into a loud snore.

"Faker. Where's a pet shrink when you need her?"

I left snob-dog on the couch and raided the fridge. I grabbed a bag of pepperoni, some Spanish cheese and multi-grain crackers, and made a small feast. I carried my platter of snack food back to the living room in time for the late night talk shows. The saltiness of the crackers and creamy Spanish cheese were the perfect partnership, a late night party in my mouth.

You'd never guess who was mentioned in the monologues.

Yep. Mona Michaels.

Apparently, *Entertainment Today*, *Inside Scoop*, and some internet gossip magazine had learned about Mona's death, and her tragic end had been broadcast to the world.

Ironically, the picture the press had chosen had been taken Emmy night. It creeped me out seeing Mona and Fluffy, side by side, with the same hairstyle and the same choker necklace. Fluffy's collar. The same one she wore now.

I leaned over and lifted Fluffy's head. Was that what the robber had been looking for? The collar had to be worth at least fifty thousand dollars. (I'm sure that was conservative.) I'd never seen Fluffy without it, but maybe, whoever had broken into Mona's didn't know Fluffy always wore her diamonds. Snob Dog eyed me, annoyed I'd interrupted her diva sleep.

I had to call Malone. I jumped up, dropping pepperoni slices on the floor. Missy stumbled over and made quick work of cleaning up my mess. I ran to my room, rummaged through my bag and found Malone's business card. I called the number. It immediately went to voicemail. (It was after midnight. I didn't expect him to answer.)

I left a brief message letting him know I'd stop by tomorrow and that I'd remembered something that might be helpful. I left out the part about having Mona's cell phone.

Fluffy yawned and stretched. I fingered the diamond heart again. It was possible the police would want it as evidence. Fluffy rested her big paw on my hand. Good Lord, she was a heavy dog.

Okay, first thing in the morning I'd stop by the shop, grab a backup collar. Then I'd make a quick stop at the police station, drop off Mona's cell and explain about the obscenely expensive collar. Then I'd meet Mona's lawyer. Maybe he'd have advice about Fluffy. It was possible the meeting was to inform me I had to hand Fluffy over to Cliff.

I felt as giddy as a beauty pageant finalist. Suddenly, tomorrow had possibilities.

Chapter Thirteen

We were on the move. The morning sun peeked through a handful of billowy clouds, teasing us with what was yet to come. The jacaranda trees were no longer in bloom yet somehow still managed to look elegant stretched toward the sky.

Another beautiful day in SoCal.

Have you ever been driving down the road, minding your own business, when suddenly someone pulls up along side of you, waving like a crazed stalker? Me either. Until today. Tricia Edwards was on the loose, and she was following me. I ignored her.

For the second day in a row, there was parking in front of Bow Wow. I nabbed a spot before some idiot could steal it from me. Tricia pulled her Mercedes in beside me, a dozen pine air fresheners swinging from her rearview mirror.

She jumped out of her car, crying erratically and waving her French manicured hands. "I had to hear about Mona from *Entertainment Today*?"

I swear, she was a *What Not To Wear* project in the flesh. Her wild, leopard-print dress and wide, studded belt was tighter than plastic wrap around Sunday leftovers no one would ever eat. It hurt my eyes to look at her.

"It wasn't my place to tell you about Mona." The dogs piled out of the Jeep. Fluffy rubbed up against me leaving a trail of dog hair on my jeans. I brushed it off as we headed for the boutique.

"Someone should have called me. I was her best friend," she whined.

Lord, she was trying. I understood she was upset by the death of her friend, but why did she think I should be the bearer of bad news? We weren't family.

I unlocked the door and strode inside. I flipped on the lights intending to grab a collar and leave, but Tricia followed me, slowing us down. I locked the door to keep out anyone else who might mistakenly believe I was open for business.

"They said you were the one who found her. What happened?"

"Fluffy found her."

The dogs and I wound through the shop while I looked for a Fluffy collar. Holy cow, there were so many choices, how did anyone decide when they were in a rush? I needed to rethink the way I laid out the accessories. Maybe I didn't need so many choices. Tricia clip-clopped behind us, never letting me forget she was there.

"You realize Jo was right," she pronounced.

"About what?" I asked distracted.

"The dream."

I turned to face her. "What about it?"

"Fluffy appeared to Jo in a dream and told her Mona would die." Tricia explained.

"And Mona believed her?" I asked, the skepticism in my voice undeniable. Was it bad I wanted to smack some sense into Tricia?

"Of course."

"Jo's a fake. Is there something I can help you with? I'm not really open."

"I've come for Fluffy." Tricia held out her privileged hand assuming I'd fork over the dog leash.

I stopped in mid-step. "Not to get personal, but are you on drugs?"

"I assume that's a rhetorical question." Her greedy brown eyes flashed with impatience.

Funny how quickly her tears had dried. "You don't even like dogs. Why would you want Fluffy?"

"I was Mona's best friend. She'd want me to care for her."

I wasn't convinced that was true. "Cliff's equal owner. If anyone should get Fluffy, it should be him." Except Mona had bitterly fought Cliff for custody, and then Cliff dropped the bombshell that he didn't want the dog. A slight wrinkle in my otherwise sound logic.

"Mona would rather die than let Cliff have Fluffy," Tricia stated.

I tilted my head sideways. "Interesting choice of words."

Tricia's flushed. "Well, it's true. It wouldn't surprise me if he was the one who killed Mona." Her grieving sadness had been replaced by catty accusations.

"Because of Fluffy?"

"Of course. He called Mona day and night, begging for money. He was always broke."

"And you know this how?" Maybe he was looking for the collar? But if that were the case, wouldn't he just take Fluffy when I'd called him? Better yet, why not take the collar?

"I'm Mona's best friend. I know everything."

I looked at Tricia. "I'm sure you don't need my advice, but I wouldn't go around accusing Cliff of murder. That could get you into a lot of trouble."

"I've done no such thing." She reached for the leash. "Give me the dog, and we'll be out of your hair."

Fluffy inched closer to me and sat on my foot. Ouch!

As much as I didn't want Fluffy, it seemed Fluffy didn't want Tricia.

I studied Tricia's standoffish stance and demanding outstretched hand, ordering me to relinquish the dog. She was probably the only one who wanted the high maintenance hairball.

I was too stubborn for my own good. I didn't appreciate being told what to do. And I really hated it when people assumed I'd do what they wanted because it was convenient for them.

There was a sudden banging on the front door. Tricia and I both jumped. The dogs immediately barked in alert and lunged toward the door. I grabbed their leashes and tied them to the counter.

"I'm closed," I shouted.

An older man hammered his fist against the door then waved an envelope in front of him.

The dogs barked louder.

"Enough. It's fine," I reassured the dogs. "I'm closed," I hollered over the noise.

He continued to beat down the door undeterred, and the dogs continued to bark.

The world had gone crazier than Uncle Wiley's pet coon.

I marched to the door and unlocked it. I opened it halfway and opened my mouth to explain I wasn't open.

"Are you Melinda Sue Langston?" his gruff voice shot out.

I was beginning to hate my name. "Yes. But I'm not open."

The dogs were still going at it in the background.

He handed me the envelope. "You've been served," he said, then fled down the street.

"What? Hey, get back here."

"You're being sued?" Tricia asked with a disturbing girlish giggle.

"Calm down. It's not a Lifetime movie of the week." I ripped open the envelope.

Sure enough. I was being sued. By Tova Randall. Seriously, how does this happen?

"Tricia, I have to go. We'll talk about Fluffy later. I have somewhere to be."

I shoved the envelope in my bag and grabbed a thick, black, snake-skinned collar with rhinestones.

"But—but, Fluffy," she stammered.

I grabbed the dogs and pushed Tricia out the door.

"Grab a martini at the Dirty Bird. We're done."

Chapter Fourteen

I'm sure by now it's obvious, I don't avoid confrontation. But I didn't have the patience to deal with Malone. As I walked up Forest, two dogs in tow, half the town either offered to take Mona's dog off my hands or spouted advice on caring for a pampered pooch like Fluffy.

The sun hid behind a handful of clouds, allowing a slight chill to settle in the air. I shivered. I formed an impromptu plan between Beach Street and the police station. If I dropped off Mona's phone at the front desk, quickly explained about the collar and then left, I'd have some extra time with Mona's lawyer. I wanted to know how Tova could sue me.

We walked inside the police station, and before the dogs and I had even reached the information counter, we had the attention of both uniformed ladies. One a body builder with a don't-waste-my-time chip on her shoulder. The other a skinny tomboy with blond curls and a really big gun.

"That's Mona's dog," the one with double D biceps said.

"Yes, it is."

"You must be Melinda." She immediately picked up the phone and paged Malone.

I shook my head and waved my hand for her to stop. "No need. I'm not here to see the detective."

"Doesn't matter," the one who couldn't have weighed more than her gun said. "He wants to see you."

Great. "I really don't have a lot of time. I have another appointment. I just wanted to—"

"Ms. Langston."

I sighed, recognizing the no-nonsense voice in an instant. "Malone."

He was just as intimidating and good looking away from his crime scene. Today he was wearing jeans, black shirt and leather jacket. He wasn't my kinda good-looking, but I could certainly see why Caro had found him appealing.

Missy lay down at my feet, drooling on my ballet flats. Fluffy growled. No drool necessary.

"Fluffy, sit." I liked her for verbalizing how I felt toward Malone.

"Come on back to my office." Said the spider to the fly.

"I'd rather not. I have another appointment."

"I'm sure you wouldn't." He left, expecting us to follow.

He's a cop. So we did.

We all traipsed down one hall and then another until we finally reached our destination. If his office were a restaurant, it'd be considered a hole in the wall, with seating for two. I'd imagined it much larger.

"Have a seat."

I chose the tan plastic chair. It was the only choice. I wasn't kidding about seating for two. "I really do have an appointment."

"Fluffy looks cleaner," he commented, keeping his back to us as he closed the door.

"Jade did a great job." I had that same heart pounding anxiety I felt in the fifth grade when I'd been summoned to the principal's office for passing notes during US History. Since then I'd had considerable experience under my pageant sash and breathed through it. *Breath in.* Whoa. Malone had had pastrami for brunch. The smell was unmistakable.

The dogs planted themselves on either side of my feet, like front yard bottlebrush shrubs. Fluffy refused to look in Malone's direction, and Missy continued to create drool pools.

"It looks like all of you are getting along." He sat in his chair opposite from me.

"Looks can be deceiving."

"I'm surprised to see you with Fluffy. I thought you were calling Cliff."

"I did. He doesn't want her."

He pushed a stack of papers to the side of his desk. "That may change."

"Look, I just stopped by to give you this." I pulled Mona's phone from my purse and slid it across his desk.

He didn't touch it. In fact, he didn't even look at it. Instead, he watched me with his commanding blue eyes. "What is it?"

"Mona's cell phone."

His cheek muscle twitched. "Why do you have it?" Calm male voices weren't always a good thing.

"When I dropped Fluffy off that night, I'd called Mona wondering where the heck she was. When I heard her phone ringing behind me on the hall table, I picked it up. I must have tossed it into my purse at the same time I put mine away. I just didn't realize it at the time."

"When *did* you realize you had potential evidence in your possession?" His stare was so intense it felt like he was trying to crawl inside my head.

I realized I was gripping the arm of the chair. I exhaled and wiggled my fingers. "Later that night. When it rang."

"Who was it?"

I could tell from the clenched jaw, I was treading on thin ice. "Tricia Edwards. Mona's best friend and business partner. She hung up before I answered, which at the time was fine by me. I didn't want to explain why I was answering Mona's phone."

"I see."

Truth be told, I didn't want explain why I had answered Mona's phone right now either. "I'm not sure that was a good thing. If I'd talked to her, she wouldn't have accosted me this morning."

"You've talked to her?"

I leaned forward, a little more confident on this subject. "About twenty minutes ago. She was upset because I hadn't told her about Mona's death. No offense, but isn't it your responsibility to notify the public? Then she demanded I hand over Fluffy. When I wouldn't, she threw Cliff under the bus saying he was broke and mad at Mona because she wouldn't give him more money."

Malone rubbed his eyes, frustrated. "What is with your family?" he bit out.

"What?"

"Do not play detective."

"I'm not," the denial was automatic. This must have been the same lecture he'd given Caro. A fat lot of good that had done him.

"You understand I'm going to verify what you've told me?"

"I'm not lying. If I had something to hide do you think I'd have brought it to you?" I made myself return his stare without blinking. But inside I was chanting for him to not ask about Darby.

Not that he had any way of knowing her number was in Mona's contact list. But he was about to. I prayed he didn't turn on the phone until after I was long gone and out of earshot.

"It's possible you erased the call history." He tapped the desk next to the phone.

"That's stupid. You're going to pull her cell records at some point."

He continued to stare at me with his unreadable face. It was becoming ridiculous. I had the urge to stick out my tongue and make faces just to see if he'd crack a smile.

"Thank you for bring the phone."

My mama had taught me to be gracious. "You're welcome. There is one more thing."

He rubbed his eyes again and muttered something under his breath that sounded like profanity. "What?"

"Officer Salinas mentioned the possibility that Mona had interrupted a robbery."

"It's one theory," he replied, guarded.

"Did you know Fluffy's collar is made of real diamonds? It's got to be worth an SUV or two."

He looked down at Fluffy. She turned her head and tipped her nose in the air, showing him her best profile.

"That's real?"

"As real as Caro's hair color."

His head snapped up, and he pinned me with a look that said I'd broached an off-limits subject. "She wears it all the time?"

I bit the inside of my cheek and fought back a smile. I was pretty sure he wasn't talking about Caro's hair. "I've never seen her without it."

"That's public knowledge?"

"To everyone except the cops."

His look said, smartass. "Fluffy was with you that night?" was what he actually said.

I couldn't take it any more. A genuine smile broke out, but I did manage to keep the giggle out of my answer. "Yes."

He wasn't impressed. He'd be a real killjoy at the family reunion. Caro would have appreciated the play on words.

"And that wasn't part of the normal routine?" he asked.

"Mona's left her dog with me before, but it wasn't a weekly event. She did it to annoy me."

He didn't say anything. He just stared at the collar. "You might want to consider a replacement and put that in a safe."

"You don't want it?"

He looked at me. "Why?"

"As evidence?"

He shook his head. "It's not evidence. Put it in a safe and get her a real collar."

"So what did you want?" I asked, suddenly reminded he'd called me into his office and not the other way around.

"You'd left me a voicemail at midnight."

"Oh. I got a little excited about the collar," I confessed.

"How is Fluffy doing?" For a second his stony expression relaxed, and I caught a glimpse of sympathy. I wasn't sure who he felt sorry for, me or the dog.

"Demanding. Does what she wants and bosses Missy around."

"I'm sure you'll work it out."

"I'm sure someone else wants this dog."

"I need you to keep her until Mona's attorney gets in touch with her new guardian."

No, no, no. "When will that happen?"

"Soon."

I waited for more information, but none came. "Not soon enough," I said.

"I have complete faith in your abilities to remain the alpha dog, Miss Langston."

He grabbed a pencil and plastic bag from his desk drawer. He used the pencil to slide the phone into the bag. The realization that I was smack dab in the middle of a murder investigation made my stomach plummet to my toes. How had that happened?

He stood, indicating our time was over. I followed his lead and gathered the dogs. He didn't ask where my next appointment was, so I didn't share that I was off to Owen Quinn's office.

Malone played everything so close to the vest. He made me feel the need to do the same.

"Let's go, dogs," I called out.

Fluffy waited for me to leave the room first (surprise) but then cut off Missy (no surprise). Missy, bless her heart, brought up the tail end without complaint.

"I guess I'll see you around." I called out over my shoulder.

"Don't forget. You gave me your word. Stay out of my investigation." Malone's booming voice chased us down the hallway.

Finding Mona's killer was the furthest thing from my mind.

Chapter Fifteen

After the meeting with Mona's lawyer, I was bursting at the seams. I needed a large chai latte and someone to talk to. Darby agreed to meet at the Koffee Klatch, a cozy local coffee shop with the best cheesecake in town. With its chic atmosphere and big comfy couches, it was the perfect place to bring the dogs and assimilate everything I'd just learned.

And I'd learned a boatload.

Fluffy, Missy and I had arrived before Darby. The deeply rich aroma saturated the air. I inhaled slowly. The smell of coffee was all I liked about the product. It didn't seem to matter how much I doctored the addicting brew, it always tasted bitter.

Missy devoured the dog treat the barista tossed her. Snob Dog watched hers hit the floor. Never one to pass up a free doggie treat, Missy ate that one, too.

We claimed the purple couch toward the back and waited. Missy sat on my lap and Fluffy sat on the floor next to us in her regal boredom. I don't think Fluffy cared for the trendy décor.

Darby blew in, a happy smile plastered on her face. Dressed in jeans, green tunic, knit scarf and flats, she waved excitedly when she saw us. She ordered her usual white mocha latte and a pumpkin bar.

Once she had her drink and snack, I motioned her over to where we were camped out.

"I can't believe you still have Fluffy." She plopped down across from me, dropping her canvas tote on the floor next to her feet. "So what's going on? You were talking so fast on the phone I could barely understand you."

She set her plate on the side table, pried off the lid on her drink and blew on the steaming liquid.

A quiet whirl of laptop computers was the only sound from the shop at the moment. I looked around making sure no one was listening. "I don't even know where to start. I just came from Owen Quinn's office."

"Who?"

"Mona's lawyer," I whispered. "Short, dark-haired fast-talker guy."

Darby leaned in. "Why did you meet with him?" She matched her tone with mine.

"Mona made me Fluffy's guardian four years ago and never changed her will."

"What?" she asked, wide-eyed.

"I had the same reaction. What in the world was she thinking?"

Darby stared at me, bewilderment frozen on her face, holding up her latte.

"Are you okay?" I asked.

She nodded and took a sip, then immediately cringed. She must have burnt her tongue.

"So you share custody with Cliff?" she asked.

"Apparently, he only had visitation rights."

"I thought they both owned her? That they had joint custody."

I sucked down some of my chai before explaining. "I saw the official document. I think they let people believe what they wanted. He doesn't have any legal claim other than he gets to visit her every Wednesday and every other weekend."

"Are you dropping off Fluffy in Dana Point?"

I shook my head. "Cliff's a complete jackass. I called him yesterday. He made it perfectly clear You-Know-Who was my problem now. And get this, he admitted he only fought for Fluffy because it hurt Mona."

"How selfish."

"Dysfunctional with a capital D, but not unexpected." We were quiet for a minute, each lost in our own thoughts.

I stroked Missy who snored delicately on my lap. I tucked a handful of napkins under her mouth to sop up her drool. Eventually, Darby nibbled on her pumpkin bar. I couldn't get over how an hour long meeting had changed my life so dramatically.

"Are you okay with all this?" I asked.

"Of course. Why wouldn't I be?"

"You didn't like Mona, and you're not a big Fluffy fan," I said. "And until something changes, she's stuck with us."

"First of all, no one is a Fluffy fan. Secondly, Mona and I were nothing more than strangers who didn't get along." She swallowed the last bite of her dessert and chased it down with some latte.

I waited until she'd finished before I shared the next tidbit of info. "Owen didn't tell me anything about the estate. But he did tell me how much You-Know-Who is worth." I nodded toward Fluffy who had finally lay down at our feet and fallen asleep.

Darby followed my gaze. "How much?"

"Just over twenty-five million dollars."

Her mouth fell open. "She left her money to her dog?"

I shook my head. "That's *Fluffy's* money, from her 'acting.' I didn't see a will. Owen needed to talk to some other people first," I said quietly.

"Cliff is going to freak out."

"I'm sure he already knows."

Darby shook her head, her blond curls bobbing in unison. "If he knew, Fluffy would already be in his possession."

Good point. "Owen did say the will stipulates Fluffy's money can only be spent on her care. Well, except for the insurance money."

"There's an insurance policy too?" she squeaked.

"Mona had two insurance policies, but Fluffy was only the beneficiary of the smaller one. He wouldn't go into detail about the other."

"I'm afraid to ask, but how much?"

"One million. Can you imagine?"

"No. I can't."

"Me either. Why in the world would she make me the caretaker?"

Darby reached over and stroked Missy. "Be careful. Once word gets out about Fluffy, Cliff will change his mind."

"Owen said if I want to be legally removed as guardian, I have to file some paperwork. The process could take a while."

"Melinda, this is weird. What are you going to do?"

"I have no idea. Fluffy's not my kind of dog. I'm sure there's someone out there who'd love her as much as Mona did." I looked over at Snob Dog. I felt compassion, but not the overwhelming connection like I had with Missy.

"What did Grey say?" Darby asked.

"He's out of town on a buying trip. I haven't told him yet. He really misses Colbalt. Maybe he'd like to foster Fluffy."

We laughed in unison. I couldn't really see Fluffy at Grey's place.

"Where's Grey this time? Somewhere exotic? I'm so jealous."

"I don't remember," I lied and looked down at Missy. Darby was sure to interpret my actions as missing Grey. I hated keeping secrets from my best friend.

We sat in silence for a few minutes sipping our drinks.

"Oh, I almost forgot. I'm being sued," I said.

Darby's head jerked up. "By who?"

"Tova. For a million dollars."

"Why?"

"Apparently, she lost a *Sports Illustrated* photo shoot because of flea bites on her legs. She is suing me for compensation for Kiki's treatment, lost wages and mental anguish."

"That's ridiculous. Who's representing her?"

"Some ambulance chaser. I'm sure as soon as he figured out I'm part of the 'Texas Montgomery' clan, he immediately saw dollar signs."

"What are you going to do?"

"I called Nigel, the family lawyer. He said it 'probably' won't go anywhere, but he did urge me to counter sue."

"For what?"

"For defamation of character."

I could only imagine Mama's reaction to this whole mess. If she thought the Miss America humiliation was bad, she'd go into hiding when she learned about a flea lawsuit.

We both looked at Fluffy who suddenly sat up and thought it was appropriate to lick herself in public.

"The world's gone crazy," Darby said on a sigh.

"You ain't just whistling Dixie."

Chapter Sixteen

For now, it seemed there was no way out of caring for Fluffy. I broke down and decided to pick up a few of her personal items. I'd called Malone, and he'd said the house was no longer a crime scene. He'd also mentioned Camilla, Mona's housekeeper, was there to inventory Mona's estate.

During our brief conversation, it had dawned on me, Malone had known all along I was Fluffy's new guardian, and he hadn't said a word. He was very good at keeping secrets.

I dropped off the dogs at home, then drove over to Mona's. I parked the Jeep (I'd switched to the hard top earlier that morning) and skedaddled to the front door.

I rang the bell and cringed. Hopefully the new owner would replace that thing.

The door opened, and there stood Camilla in slacks and blouse. She looked very attractive. I wondered if she'd burned the unflattering black uniform Mona had insisted she wear.

"Hi, Camilla. I came by to pick up some of Fluffy's things."

"Miz Melinda. You bring Fluffy?" She stepped back and welcomed me inside.

"I left her at my place. I didn't think bringing her home was good for her. Did you know Mona named me Fluffy's guardian?"

"Si. I hear." She closed the door. "I have Fluffy's things for you." Her light accent echoed throughout the palatial foyer.

I followed her to the sunroom. Sure enough, it was packed to the top of the white crown molding with Fluffy's belongings. The luxurious couches and tables were covered with boxes, crates and leaning stacks of dog stuff. There was more inventory here than I carried during tourist season.

Brushes, combs, hair clips, hair products, dog food, Waterford crystal dog bowls. Blankets, toys, CDS, DVDS, clothing, a dog bed, pillows, pictures. You get the idea.

Lord have mercy, there was no way it would all fit in my Jeep. "I don't need all of this." I waved my hand at the mess in front of us.

"These are Fluffy's belongings. You must take them."

"I'd have to rent a moving truck to get this back to my place. Even then I wouldn't have room for everything."

She nodded. "Miz Mona spoiled Fluffy."

Or Mona was a hoarder. Either way it was obvious she was two sandwiches short of a picnic.

"Tell me what I absolutely must take." I refastened my ponytail, securing all the stray hairs around my face and sighed. "Everything else can stay here until I figure out what I'm going to do."

"You not keep Fluffy?" her accent grew more pronounced. She shook her head and pointed a finger at me. "You have to. Miz Mona trusted you to keep Fluffy safe."

"What do you mean, safe?"

She crossed herself. "She trusted you."

"How do you know?"

She just stared at me with that knowing look that said people in her position knew more than they should, but she wasn't one to gossip.

"You might as well talk. Mona's dead. She can't punish you for spillin' the beans."

She wrung her hands, obviously nervous to repeat Mona's words. "She said you were impulsive, had no fashion sense, and sabotaged your one shot at success."

Mona had a lot to say. Just because I preferred jeans and t-shirts (today's shirt read, *Sit Happens*), didn't mean I wasn't fashionable. I didn't argue the other two. They were pretty accurate.

"She also said you wouldn't ever use her Fluffy."

Well heck, when did I get so predictable?

"That's all nice and very Mona-like, but that doesn't convince me Fluffy's in danger or why I'm her only option for a well-adjusted life."

Camilla regarded me with a stubborn set to her mouth and refused to say more.

"I'm not taking all of this home. I came for a brush, food and hair product."

Camilla was suddenly in motion. "You must take her favorite bowl. And pictures. She can't forget Miz Mona. Oh, and home movies."

She was like a wild woman piling Fluffy's belongings at my feet.

"I have a Jeep not a U-Haul," I reminded her.

"She likes filtered water and her bathrobe. Nail clippers, toothbrush, breath mints, clean-up bags, vitamins . . ."

"Whoa. Hold on there."

Camilla stopped in the middle of tossing the plastic bottle of vitamins.

"Give me the bowl, brush, bathing products and food."

"No pictures?" she looked pleadingly at me.

"Fine. Pick one," I relented.

"And a home movie?"

"You're pushing it."

She hid a small smile as she gathered the few items I agreed to take, loaded them into a huge designer dog bed.

"You and Fluffy get along. It will be good. You see." She patted my arm.

"Whatever you say, Camilla. I can see you're in charge now."

I pretended not to see her sneak a movie, a large envelope (which was probably full of pictures) and a doggie cookbook on the pile. I didn't want to break her heart, but I wasn't cooking for Mona's dog.

With Camilla's help we carried everything to the Jeep and somehow managed to shove it all inside. (At the last minute, she'd insisted I take all of Fluffy's tiaras and a small safe to store them. The dog actually had a safe.) I left with my Fluffy items and headed home. I couldn't worry about the mess I was leaving behind. I had a feeling I was driving into an even bigger one.

It had been a long and stressful day. My neck was stiff, and my back was sore. I'd cleaned out the guest room (AKA junk room) and made room for Fluffy and her belongings. I left a number of items in a small box in the closet, planning to get to them later.

So far Fluffy was unimpressed with the setup and continued to nap on my bed. I crossed my fingers that by bedtime she'd prefer her own room.

A long soak in the tub was in order. But first I wanted my special peanut butter cookie and a mug of milk. My mouth watered in anticipation.

Missy and Fluffy staked out the kitchen doorway in a doggie trance waiting for me to drop dough. I'm sure the smell of freshly baked cookies was making their mouths drool. I know mine was.

I'd just pulled the last batch from the oven when my cell phone rang, interrupting my baking party. Mama's name flashed on the screen. It rang three more times before I picked up.

"Hello, Mama."

"I can't believe you let me hear about Mona on the news. You were brought up better than that, Sugar." Her confident voice and teased, bottle-blond hair carried across the miles.

I pulled out a hands-free ear bud from my junk drawer and continued transferring cookies onto the cooling rack.

"I've been a little preoccupied. How's Daddy?" I asked.

My daddy was a saint. John "Jack" Langston had managed to stay married to Mama for almost thirty-five years. Mama had trapped Daddy when she was nineteen. Daddy didn't seem to mind. (He said no one ever forced him to do anything he didn't want to. I believed him.) Mama acted like it hadn't really happened. But my brother Mitch existed, and at times I believed he paid the price for Mama's reckless decision.

"He's fine. What happened to Mona?" she asked. No, *demanded.*

"She was murdered."

"Oh, Melinda. Why are you so difficult? You know what I'm talking about. Who did it? Was it an intruder or someone she knew? What happened?"

I dumped the dirty cookie sheets into the sink. I took a deep breath of patience, keeping in mind they were childhood friends. "The police don't confide in me, Mama."

"I heard Fluffy was the one to find her and called 9-1-1."

I smiled. "Ah, no. Fluffy can't use a phone. That was me."

"You found her?"

"No, that was Fluffy."

She was quiet for a second. I took that opportunity to fill the mixing bowl with water.

"Who has the dog, Melinda?" she asked, exasperated.

I looked at Fluffy whose eyes begged for cookies. "Me."

"You already have a dog." She didn't shriek. That wasn't acceptable from someone with her pedigree. But her normally soft Texas accent thickened.

"A number of people have more than one dog. Mona thought I should be guardian. So Fluffy's here, either hogging my bed or sleeping on my couch." I poured myself a mug of milk.

"Why would you ever let her share your bed? Doesn't she have her own? What if she has fleas? Really, Melinda, don't you think about these things?"

The vexation in her voice drummed in my ears. It was time to change the subject—or hang up. "What happened between the two of you? You and Mona."

"Back in the day, Mona was wild and fun. But, if you got on her bad side, she could be very nasty," she stated, more than a little vinegar in her tone. Then in the next breath, she changed her mind. "That's all water under the bridge. It's neither here nor there."

"Mama—"

"It's not important, Melinda."

It was to me. I grabbed a warm cookie and my milk, and sat at the breakfast bar. The dogs followed and staked out the floor next to my stool.

"What did she say when she called you?" I asked.

"Honey, we haven't talked in years. Why would she call me?"

There was no hesitation in Mama's voice. A fire burned in my gut. Mona had lied. "She said some horrible things about you at the Fur Ball," *even if they were true*, "and I lost my temper."

"Oh, Melinda Sue. Why must you be so reckless? What have you done now?"

I broke a peanut butter cookie in half and dunked it in the milk. "Nothing you'd approve of, I can promise you that much. The only reason I'm probably not a suspect in her murder is because I have an alibi."

"Shh. Don't talk like that."

"Well, someone hated her so much they killed her." I popped my pre-bedtime snack into my mouth. Delicious.

"You're assuming Mona was killed out of hate. It could just as easily been because of jealousy or love or money."

I tapped the side of the mug. "Which of those would Cliff fall under?"

"All of them. That heathen is as crooked as a snake. You're not giving him that dog, are you?"

I looked to my right at Fluffy. "He doesn't want her."

"Of course not."

"Why did Mona marry him in the first place?"

"Cliff is very charming when he's not . . . knee deep in his vices."

Leave it to Mama to skirt around calling Cliff a drunk. I chowed down the other half of the cookie.

"Enough about Mona and that dreadful topic, have you heard from Mitchell lately?" She tried to sound nonchalant, but anyone who knew my mother would recognize that slight lift of her voice on my brother's name.

The real reason for her late night call. It was only eight-thirty in California, but back in Dallas, it was ten-thirty. Past former Miss Texas' bedtime.

"Not recently."

My brother was an architect working in Las Vegas. He specialized in luxury hotels and was hardly at his Dallas home. Mitch felt like the black sheep of the family. He wasn't. He just picked up on Mama's guilt.

To be fair, he was the perfect child. I, on the other hand, was probably why my parents' hair had turn prematurely grey under that bottle color.

"Your big brother is hiding something."

I broke a second cookie in half and dunked it in the milk. "Because he hasn't called?" He'd probably talked to Daddy instead. But if we didn't talk to Mama once a week, she was convinced we were hiding something. The problem was, we probably were.

"I was just talking to him. He was as chatty as a magpie."

That *was* suspicious. Langston men were not talkative. "What did he say?" I asked with my mouthful.

"He was still in Las Vegas working on his hotel. He's thinking about buying a house there. He wouldn't be home for a while, but not to worry, he was fine."

I swallowed. Mitch never shared details about his life. Any details Mama knew, she'd have learned from the media.

"Are you sure he told you this? You're not assuming? You didn't read about it somewhere?"

"I know the difference between Mitchell's voice and mine. Call him and find out what's going on."

"Mama, Mitch is a grown man. He doesn't have to answer to the family every time he does something you don't like." But of course I was going to call. He may be hiding something from our mama, but odds were he'd tell me.

"You'll call him. You know you'd feel terrible if something happened to your only brother, and you didn't help him."

I hated it when she played the guilt card.

Missy, who was still under my stool, rolled over and exposed her belly. I continued to rub her. "If he doesn't want you to know something, I'm not going to tattle on him."

"You will tell me. Or I'll call Kat and convince her it's time to visit y'all."

Holy crapola. This was serious business. Mama and Aunt Kat,

together. Here. Caro would kill me.

For a threat, it worked.

I'd call Mitch. Dependin' on what he had to say would dictate if I needed to make another exception and call Caro. It was only fair to give my cousin warning her mama was on her way for a visit.

It had been a few of days since Mona's death. The three of us had settled into somewhat of a routine. There were no leads on Mona's murderer. At least not that the police were sharing with the rest of the town. But there was plenty of gossip.

I'd called Mitch, and Mama was right, he was chatty. He didn't spill his dirty little secret, but my sisterly intuition told me he had one. I let it go. If he were really in trouble, he'd have told me. Now it was about letting Mama squirm.

"Let's go, girl," I called out to Missy. She happily plodded behind me.

I thought Fluffy might follow. She'd seen the morning routine often enough, but she was hiding out either on my bed or on the couch.

She still wasn't interested in her own room. I couldn't figure her out.

I hopped into the shower and sang my favorite Sting song at the top of my lungs. Missy joined in during the chorus. I'm sure our screeching and howling was hard on Fluffy's ears. We certainly wouldn't win any singing contests.

Our duet was interrupted by my blaring cell phone. I shut off the water and hopped out of the shower. Rivulets of water dripped on the hardwood floor.

"Ms. Langston. Owen Quinn. I-wanted-to-make-you-aware . . . Mona-Michael's-funeral-is-today."

How could someone talk so fast and not be winded?

Earlier in the week, the rumor of a possible funeral had spread through the community. Since I hadn't heard it directly from anyone I trusted, I'd dismissed it. I patted my face dry with the corner of the towel. "I didn't think there'd be one."

"The body won't be released in time, but Ms. Michaels had a precise timeline and this is what she wanted."

Dictating our lives from the grave. No surprise.

"Fluffy's to attend."

"O-kay," I dragged out the word while I contemplated what that meant to me. "So am I supposed to drop her off?" There was silence on the other end. "I'm joking. What time?"

He filled me in on the details at neck-breaking speed (2:00 pm at the Presbyterian Church), then we hung up.

"What does a dog wear to a funeral?"

I knew what I was going to wear.

Grandma Tillie's brooch.

Chapter Seventeen

It was gone.

Damn. I pulled down two extra-large wicker baskets from the top shelf in my closet. I knew there'd be hell to pay. Caro had been livid when I'd stolen the brooch out from under her nose. Somehow she'd found the opportunity to return the gesture.

Caro was getting better at breaking and entering. And I was getting worse at hiding my loot.

I dumped out the basket contents. Ten (okay, more like twenty) handbags covered my bed. Coach, Fendi, Chanel, Marc Jacobs, Prada, Alexander Wang and Chloe'. Hobos, totes, shoulder and evening. Neutrals, blacks, purple, plaid, blue, green and metallic. I loved my bags.

I'd thought hiding the brooch in a handbag, on the top shelf of my walk-in closet, was the perfect hiding spot.

I was wrong.

I was missing a bag. Not just any bag, but an Alexander McQueen feather-fringed box-clutch with a fantastic gold and amber crystal skull clasp.

I'd been so wrapped up in Fluffy's issues, I'd let down my guard. Dang. Dang. Dang.

Fluffy meandered over to the bed and sniffed the bags. She settled on the Chloe' brown leather tote. She had good taste. It was one of my favorites. To be honest, I loved them all; why else would I buy them?

Fluffy studied me as she slowly grabbed the shoulder strap between her teeth.

"What are you doing?" I asked, reaching for the bag.

She yanked the purse out of my grasp and rushed out of the room. I gave chase, yelling at her, "Get back here. Drop the bag."

She ran through the house, Missy and I right behind her.

"Bark. Bark."

That was Missy.

"Don't make me chase you. Fluffy, you get back here."

Fluffy stopped in the middle of the living room and faced me in a pounce position, hairy butt in the air. Missy and I blocked her exit toward the hallway.

It was a stare down.

This was the time she picked to act like a dog? I needed a distraction. Or bribe.

"Treat?" I asked.

Missy immediately sat and barked.

"Not you, girl. Fluffy, do you want a treat?" I walked toward the kitchen, keeping an eye on the dogs. "I have doggie cookies. This one looks like pizza." I lifted the rump from my Golden Retriever cookie jar on the counter.

Fluffy didn't move. Missy bumbled into the kitchen and sat at my feet and immediately produced a puddle of drool. I tossed her a cookie.

Snob Dog laid down.

"Do you want one?" I held it in front of me as I slowly made my way to her. She stared at me like I was an idiot. "I'll trade you, the purse for the treat."

I tossed the cookie a couple of feet from Fluffy. She dropped the purse and sniffed the treat. I grabbed my Chloe' tote and checked it for damage. Other than dog slobber, it was fine.

"I didn't think I'd need to tell you this, but my purses and shoes are off limits."

Fluffy ate her treat and then barked.

"I hope taking you to the funeral isn't something I'm going to regret."

While the dogs ate their snack I decided I wasn't about to attend the shindig of the year alone. I called for reinforcements.

Darby agreed to play chaperone to Fluffy and me. I couldn't help but wonder who else was just finding out about the funeral. I hoped Caro made an appearance. I wanted my brooch back.

Two hours later Darby, Fluffy and I zoomed down PCH. It was a drab kinda afternoon, overcast and gloomy. Perfect for a funeral.

Not sure what to wear, I'd settled on a belted cashmere dress sans Grandma Tillie's brooch. Fluffy sported her diamond collar. I'd brought her tiara, but hadn't decided if I'd make her wear it. Darby thought I should have left it in the safe.

"Do you think anyone will be there?" Darby adjusted the seatbelt over her chocolate-colored wrap dress.

"Well, we'll be there. I'm sure Tricia will show."

"What about Cliff?"

"Does the funeral home serve Scotch?"

I pulled into the church parking lot. It was packed. We drove in circles before we found a place down 2nd Street. I checked my watch, worried we were late. It was only one thirty.

"I guess that answers that." I turned off the Jeep and set the emergency brake.

A group of ladies (and I only use that term because I can't come up with something more accurate at the moment) toddled past us and up the street in their five-inch heels, hair extensions, and faces pulled back until they looked like Halloween masks. I didn't recognize a single one.

Funeral crashers.

"It's a chapter out of *The Idiot's Guide On How to Climb The Social Ladder*," I said.

"Leave the tiara," Darby deadpanned.

We grabbed our purses and climbed out of the Jeep. The three of us walked up the sidewalk side by side, hair blowing in the afternoon breeze. Nose and tail in the air, Fluffy, the runway supermodel of dogs, owned us all.

We made our way up the street in silence. I didn't know about Darby, but I was preparing for what we'd find inside the beautifully dramatic church.

The Spanish influence was obvious in its off-white stucco walls and red tile roof. Its wrought iron balconies and mini shrub mazes hinted at a blush of romance. It seemed a better fit for a wedding than a funeral. The recently renovated super-sized bell tower made me think of Mona's doorbell.

The three of us climbed the steps and entered the church behind the latest gaggle of gossip mongers. The lobby, equally as beautiful as the outside, spilled over with extravagantly dressed bodies and hushed voices. Their faux reverence wasn't out of mourning, but scandalous chit-chat. It was sad and pathetic, and I actually felt badly for Mona.

It didn't take long before I spotted a handful of the usual suspects you'd find at a society event. The mayor and the city council had staked out one corner of the room. Probably rehashing which streets to tear apart and repave next. Not that they'd finished repairing the first round of destruction yet.

I scanned the open room for Owen, looking for a little guidance on where Fluffy should sit. Out of the corner of my eye Tricia appeared dressed in all black, including a pillbox hat with a stack of huge black organza leaves dangling in front of her face. She looked like the widow and not a grieving best friend. It was creepy.

Tova swaggered inside in a bright pink sheath dress looking like Elle Woods, only instead of Legally Blonde she was Lethally Blonde. She maneuvered an enormous leopard print handbag around the small crowd hovering around the guest book. If I had to guess, which I didn't because it was obvious, her bag hid Kiki.

As much as I wanted to deal with her immediately, it wasn't appropriate (again, those dang southern manners). But once those church bells rang, it was game on.

"Darby, I drank too much tea before we left. Can you keep Fluffy for a second?"

"Sure."

She accepted the leash, and I patted Fluffy's head. I made quick work of locating the ladies' room. It was empty so I had my choice of stalls.

I was just about to flush when the restroom door opened and an argument in progress entered.

"Don't threaten me." That voice was on a slow simmer.

"You misunderstood." Overly sweet foghorn voice.

"No, I don't believe I did. You said if I didn't help you, I'd be sorry. That's a threat."

Ah, thank you Captain Obvious.

It had to be Tricia and Jo. I peeked through the crack to see what they were doing.

Wow. It sounded like Jo, but it sure didn't look like her.

She'd actually brushed her bushy red hair and pulled on a dress. I pressed my face up against the stall door, straining for a less obstructed view. Sure enough, navy blue, cowl-neck dress and closed toe pumps.

She was a hot mess.

Tricia studied herself in the mirror as she reapplied her red lipstick. "I'd think you'd have enough to deal with. I heard the police questioned you about your part in Mona's murder."

Jo closed the space between them, making it difficult to see her face. "I warned her someone was going to kill her. I had nothin' else to do with her death." The slight tremor in her voice hinted at repressed anxiety.

"That's not true, and we both know it. Mona told me all about—" she stopped abruptly and stared at my partial reflection in the mirror.

"Who's in here?"

Dang. I held my breath. I wanted to know what Mona had told her.

"I can see your eye. Come out." Since Mona had died, Tricia had appointed herself as the new Queen of Bossy.

I emerged from the stall. "Don't let me keep you from arguing." I washed and dried my hands, wanting to get out of the line of fire now that there was nothing good to overhear.

Jo squinted and glared at me. "You were eavesdropping," she accused.

I smoothed my dress and made a beeline for the door. "Nice visiting, but I've got a dog waiting for me."

Yikes. That was wild. I quickly found my way back to where I'd left Darby and Fluffy.

"What took you so long?" Darby practically threw the leash at me.

I nodded over my shoulder toward Jo, who'd followed me out of the ladies' room. "I was trapped in the bathroom. I'll explain later."

"I can't wait to hear this one."

Fluffy allowed me to lead as we made our way toward the inner sanctum of the building. She wasn't honoring our agreement. She was finished with the crowd and ready to go home. I mean my place.

Lord have mercy. I caught a glimpse of my brooch heading inside the sanctuary. I almost gave myself whiplash as I turned in Caro's direction.

"Hey, you stole that from me."

"I retrieved what was *rightfully* mine," her soft steely voice matched my inner resolve.

Damn. Darn. (We were in church. I had to watch my damns.) She looked good in her black Chanel dress.

"Uh, Mel, this isn't really the place to have a smack down with your cousin." Darby, the voice of reason.

"Later," I promised.

"Of course, Sugar."

Caro's smug serene smile bugged the crapola out of me. I watched her glide to her seat in the back, all beauty pageant poise and world peace sincerity. Oh, I'd get my brooch back.

"No offense, but that's one ugly piece of jewelry. Maybe you should just let her have it," Darby whispered.

"No way."

We stood at the back of the sanctuary. The interior of the church was gorgeous. Hand-carved wooden pews, a dozen or so arches and stained-glass windows to the right and left, it all lent to the feel of a spiritual journey. But that wasn't what surprised me.

The service décor was bare. A handful of modest flower arrangements and a couple of potted plants decorated the front. The portrait of Fluffy and Mona that had hung in her bedroom was now propped up next to her empty bronze casket.

It was tasteful. Nowhere near a true representation of Mona's preference. Who was running the show? Owen? Good thing Mona couldn't see the backdrop of her last performance.

Tricia brushed past us and down the aisle and toward the front, shoulders thrown back and in a hurry. Cliff Michaels was right behind her and hadn't bothered to dress up. He looked every bit the tourist in his wrinkled white linen pants and bowling shirt. The gentleman with him was dressed marginally better. His clothes weren't wrinkled but just as casual. They took the pew behind Tricia.

Darby, Fluffy and I were next.

I could feel all eyes on us. I'm pretty sure the look on my face said don't-talk-to-me. If a dog could have a look on its face, it was the same. Fluffy was in her element; she was born to be the center of attention.

As we walked past the guests, I realized it was as if anyone who'd ever held a grudge against Mona was gathered in the same place at once.

Jo, Cliff, Darby, Tova, and me. If I were the cops—

Speaking of the Malone. I spotted him sitting discreetly in the back. He'd exchanged his t-shirt for a dress shirt and tie. He'd picked the opposite side of the church as Caro. Coincidence? I don't think so.

Out of the corner of my eye I caught him watching people. Caro included. She was doing a respectable of job of ignoring him. They must have had words.

We sat toward the middle. I made Fluffy sit in the aisle. I wasn't familiar on the proper protocol for a dog in church, but I bet Fluffy on the furniture was a big no-no.

The service was brief and semi-painless. The only true awkward moment was when the officiator asked if anyone wanted to speak. Tricia was too distraught. She'd made sure everyone saw her tears and heard her whimpers. I quickly realized no one was interested.

Darby looked at me, and I shook my head. Mama said if you didn't have anything nice to say, keep your trap shut. That's exactly what I was going to do. I found it interesting no one else had anything nice to say either.

After a minute or two of awkward silence, the service was

pronounced over. Thank goodness. Fluffy had a bad case of gas, and I needed some fresh air.

Chapter Eighteen

We dashed outside and found a spot for Fluffy to have some privacy under a jacaranda tree behind the church. I pulled out a Doody Bag from my purse and removed all evidence that she'd ever been there.

"Did you notice Mona's intimate circle of friends didn't even look at each other?" Darby sounded as if she had suddenly caught a case of the sniffles.

"We should be thankful. Mean and cunning is a dangerous combination."

I checked her out surreptitiously under my lashes. Yup, she'd been crying. Kindhearted Darby. It was sweet. I didn't want to embarrass her, so I ignored it.

We found a Dumpster in the back of the parking lot and tossed our obscenely large Fluffy gift inside. I dug out a bottle of hand sanitizer from my bag and squeezed a dollop into my palm.

I'd been watching for Caro since the end of the service, but she must have escaped out a side door. I hadn't seen the one other person I needed to set straight either.

"Have you seen Tova?" I asked.

"Not since we left the church," Darby replied.

We doubled back to the front where a group of phony mourners had amassed.

"Let's drown our sorrows at the Kitty Cat Club," someone suggested.

For those not in the know, the Kitty Cat Club was the only bar in Laguna where you could catch a drag show on the weekend. Word on the street was the performance was pretty decent.

I was ready to head back to the Jeep, but Fluffy towed me in Cliff's direction, who was talking on his cell as he trudged toward the parking lot.

"Really? You want to see him?" Fluffy continued to pull on the leash. "Oh, all right." I couldn't believe she missed the jerk.

I turned to tell Darby where we were heading, but she was in a deep conversation with Don Furry. Poor guy was probably still upset about the missing ARL donation.

As we approached Mona's ex, I could hear his side of the conversation.

"I heard you." Cliff's words took on a menacing tone. "I don't have it right now. She didn't leave me the damn dog."

I slowed my steps. Fluffy pulled against the leash to walk faster.

"Once I get my hands on that dog I'll be able to pay you back." He shoved his hand in his front pocket.

Of course, now he wanted Fluffy. Because he owed someone money? I'd love to know whom he was talking to.

"I just need a couple more days," he insisted. He swore and hung up.

He whipped around, anger and fear clearly imprinted on his face.

"Hey, Cliff. Nice ceremony. I hope you don't mind, Fluffy wanted to say hello," I pretended, as if I hadn't overheard his conversation.

Fluffy nuzzled his knee, and Cliff absently patted her head. "I want my dog," he demanded.

Instinctively, I took a step back. "I don't think so."

"I have custody every Wednesday." He wrapped his fingers around the leash. His greedy gaze landed on Fluffy's collar.

Uh-oh. "That was days ago. You weren't interested. Besides, you have visitation, not custody."

Fluffy tensed and pulled back from his grasp.

Cliff narrowed his black coffee eyes and rubbed his unshaved jaw with his free hand. The little hairs on the back of my neck took notice and warned me to proceed with caution.

I gripped the leash tighter. "I know the truth. As Fluffy's legal guardian, I was supplied with the facts. The *real* facts."

"It doesn't change that it's a court order. You have to give me the dog. I have to have the dog," he slurred. He tugged the leash, and both Fluffy and I jumped. Fluffy yelped as I accidentally stepped on her paw.

"Sorry, girl."

Malone appeared out of nowhere. "That's in interesting choice of words, Mr. Michaels. Why do you *have* to have Fluffy?"

Malone glowered at Cliff's grip. Mona's ex let go of the leash. I immediately stepped out of his reach, keeping Fluffy close to my side. My mouth felt like the Texas plains.

Beads of sweat popped out on Cliff's forehead. "Mona owes me that much. We had an agreement." His voice rose.

"Sounds like she stiffed you. Some people get desperate when they don't get what they think they deserve," I said.

Cliff looked wildly between me and Malone. Fluffy growled. This wasn't good.

"I'm not desperate," he shouted. "I just want what's mine. What Mona promised."

"How much money do you owe?" Malone's calm voice and demeanor belied the watchful tension he radiated.

"Keep your nose out of my business." The hatred etched on Cliff's face made me catch my breath.

With one last sneer, he stormed off toward his Land Rover.

I looked at Malone. "Lord have mercy. He killed Mona."

"Stay out of it," he barked.

My heart raced. "I'm not in anything. I'm just telling you he killed Mona." Then I remembered the argument in the bathroom. "Unless it was Jo."

"What?" His irritated growl rivaled Fluffy's.

"You know, Jo O'Malley, the pet psychic. I just overheard her threatening Tricia in the ladies room before the service started."

"About what?" he asked reluctantly.

"I'm not really sure. If I had to guess, it was about Mona."

"Don't guess. Stay out of it." He turned on his heel and walked away.

Fluffy and I chased after him. It was difficult to keep up in my four-inch Louboutin pumps. "But what else could she be talking about? What if Jo murdered Mona?" I asked.

"Are you and your cousin hard of hearing? Stay out of it." He didn't look over his shoulder. Or slow down.

"But what if Mona realized Jo was a fraud and threatened to expose her? People kill each other over that kind of stuff."

"Cut back on the drama cable shows."

"You know it's true. People have killed because their reputations and businesses are about to be destroyed."

He froze. I ran into his back. Dang, he was buff under that leather jacket. He whipped around. I could clearly see his unreadable face.

"You mean like you and your friend Darby?" he asked quietly.

"You know I didn't do it. And Darby certainly didn't have anything to do with Mona's death," I denied.

"How can you be so sure?"

Ok, so he'd checked out the cell phone and had probably found a way to listen to her message. This wasn't looking good for my buddy. "What did she gain from Mona's death? Nothing."

He looked like he wanted to say something but stopped himself. "Stay out of this, or I'll have you arrested."

I held up my hand. "I'm not a part of it. I'm only here because Mona dictated, from beyond her grave, that Her Majesty attend the service."

"Stay out of it," he shot me the evil eye, "or I'll throw you in jail."

News flash. I'd already spent a night in jail.

It had happened shortly after *The Incident* when I was trying to prove I was my own person. Public intoxication had landed me in the city jail for twenty-four hours. Daddy had refused to bail me out. He was stubborn that way.

After a few hours I'd gotten used to the stench. Sleeping on the cold, concrete floor between the other drunks and a hooker named Daisy, I'd realized I could survive just about anything.

Bring it on, Malone. A short stay behind posh Laguna Beach bars doesn't scare me. But his innuendo about Darby, now that had me worried.

Our little trio regrouped. We meandered toward the Jeep chatting about the funeral and my suspicion that either Cliff or Jo had killed Mona. I sugarcoated the confrontation between Cliff, Malone and me. I completely left out Malone's suspicion about Darby.

We were guessing how much Cliff owed when, out of nowhere, a black SUV jumped the curb and sped into the church parking lot. It slammed to a stop and parked behind Cliff's Land Rover.

A nervous Cliff stood next his vehicle. The SUV driver's window rolled down a crack. I stopped.

"Mel, what's going on?" Darby asked.

"Hold on." I strained to hear across the parking lot, hoping to catch a portion of the conversation. I couldn't hear anything, but I could tell by Cliff's stiff stance and balled fists he was angry.

From the corner of my eye, Malone appeared and casually headed in Cliff's direction. The driver must have seen him, too, and wasn't interested in a chat.

The tinted window rolled up, and the vehicle squealed out of the parking lot, leaving behind a distraught Cliff and an irritated and suspicious Malone. Oh, and about two feet of tire rubber.

"Cliff's implicating himself further by the minute," I said. Darby had nothing to worry about.

Chapter Nineteen

Grey came home the next day. It was a great reunion full of Chinese takeout, foot rubs and a couple of glasses of Cabernet Sauvignon. Darby had been a dear and offered to dog-sit Fluffy for the night. I let her.

Missy, Grey and I camped out on the patio with a devastatingly beautiful view of the Pacific. Grey lived in the Laguna Beach highlands referred to as Top of the World.

I loved experiencing sunset from his place. It was as if I could reach out and skim my fingers along the pastel hues of the sky. I swear there were times I could smell the scent of the setting sun.

The tension that had surrounded us the last time we were together was gone. Tonight it was about reconnecting, and I loved it.

"So how was the funeral?" he asked, stretched out on a chaise lounge in jeans and a sweater.

From my matching chair, I rolled to my side so I was facing him. He turned his head in my direction. His intelligent green eyes watched me lazily. I set my wine glass on the flagstone.

"Crazy. Jo and Tricia were arguing in the women's bathroom. Cliff demanded that I give him Fluffy. Malone threatened to throw me in jail. And Caro had the audacity to show up wearing *my* brooch."

"What did you do?"

"I wanted to rip it off her chest—"

He chuckled. "Why did Malone threaten to toss you in jail? Again."

"Oh." I smiled sheepishly. The night grew chilly. I tugged at the bottom of my sweater to cover my behind. "He thinks I'm poking my nose into his investigation because I told him either Jo or Cliff killed Mona. I'm leaning toward Cliff."

"Last week you thought he was a loser."

"He's still a loser. But I overheard him talking on his cell phone. He owes someone money, and, from the sound of it, it's a lot. Then he threatened me because I wouldn't give him Fluffy. And when Darby and I were leaving, we saw him involved in a super intense conversation he didn't want Malone to hear."

The air that had been relaxed and calm now sparked with a new energy. The length of Grey's body tensed, down to his bare feet. "Stay away from him. Let the police handle it."

I didn't want to ruin the mood. "Let's change the subject," I suggested.

Grey rotated to his side and reached for me. He kissed the back of my hand, adjusted my sapphire engagement ring. "When were you going to tell me you had Mona's phone?" his voice was deceptively gentle.

I withdrew from his grasp, uncertain of how much he knew and how much was a guess. "You knew?"

"It's my job to notice details. Why are you keeping secrets from me?"

My pulse quickened. I sensed his uneasiness at broaching the subject. It was time to clear the air. I quickly explained everything, including Darby's number being programmed into the phone. "I wanted to talk to her before I turned the phone over to Malone. I knew if I told you, you'd want me to give the phone directly to the police."

"You didn't confide in me because you didn't trust me." His jaw was so rigid it looked like it was about to splinter. He was hurt by what he thought was my lack in confidence of him.

"It wasn't about me trusting you," I picked my words carefully, wanting to be truthful but not cause further upset. "I knew you'd be angry if I kept the phone. And I didn't want to lie. I'm sorry. I do trust you."

"But you don't want me telling you what to do."

That was the truth staring us both in the face. I brushed the hair away from his forehead, looking for an excuse to touch him, to reassure us both. "You've always known that about me." I shot a quick self-deprecating grin at him. "That says more about me than you."

It was silent except for Missy's snoring and the cricket concert. The mood shifted again as we found our footing.

"Why did Darby call Mona?" he asked.

It was difficult to look Grey in the face and answer. "I'm not sure. When I asked, she made up a story."

"She lied."

I nodded, not wanting to speak the words out loud. But it didn't make it untrue. My friend had lied to me.

He sighed, and I felt him let go of whatever emotion he'd been grappling with. Grey never held a grudge. "Mel, do you think she had something to do with Mona's death?"

"No."

"She lied to you."

"I know. But I'm certain she had a really good reason. Maybe Mona was holding some secret over her head. I lie to her every day about you. I can't be too upset at her. Not yet anyway. I did promise you'd help if she needed a lawyer."

"Melinda."

"What? You can't recommend someone?" I smiled, knowing he'd do what he could. That's who he was.

He flopped to his back. "Let's hope she doesn't need my help."

"Can we change the subject for real? How was your trip?" I asked.

"Educational."

Whatever that meant. "Did you bring back any fake art?"

He looked at me funny, as if it was his turn to make a crucial decision.

I laughed softly. "You know I only call it that because it's your cover."

The "trips" were his cover for leaving town, but his art gallery, ACT (the acronym stood for Art Crime Team. Clever, huh?), was the real deal. He excelled at plucking new artists out of obscurity and launching them into the spotlight. If he ever retired from superhero status, he had a whole other career waiting for his undivided attention.

He sat up, straddling the lounge chair. His body vibrated with action and his eyes full of life. "Actually, I did bring back real 'fake art.'"

I sat up too, hugging my knees to my chest. "Forgeries? Can I see them?" excitement bubbled as I realized he was talking about work. His real work.

"They may be commissioned copies. No, I can't show you."

"I thought that was illegal."

"You can have a replica," he explained. "You can't pass off a replica as the original."

"Is that what was happening?"

"That remains to be seen."

I regarded him seriously. He looked as if he'd been set free, and I felt off kilter, unsettled. I couldn't pinpoint the emotions swarming inside. "Why are you suddenly sharing with me?"

He shrugged. "You were interested. I'm trying."

I gently moved my wine glass from the ground to the side table between our chairs. I joined him on his lounge and snuggled up against him. My heart hammered against my chest.

"I love you, Grey Donovan."

"I love you, too." There was no smile in his voice, just honest sincerity.

I rested my head on his chest and could hear the pounding of his heart.

"I was serious about Cliff," he spoke into my hair. "He's dangerous. Stay away from him."

It was a cool Sunday morning, and the early fog rolled in like the smoke from Granddad Montgomery's cigars. Missy and I had just wrapped up a Doga class (yoga with your dog and way more intense than *Mommy and Doggie Yoga*) on Main Beach. A light transparent mist settled on my arms. I felt refreshed and ready for the day.

Fluffy was still with Darby. Dressed in my yoga clothes and my hair pulled back into a messy ponytail, Missy and I zipped over to Darby's rented cottage. Her place managed to be both whimsical yet practical. It fit her personality perfectly.

I left Missy in the Jeep with the windows down. She'd managed to get half of her stocky body out the window, panting with excitement. She seemed to like Fluffy.

I rounded the corner of the walkway, brushing past a cluster of lofty periwinkle delphiniums. I knocked on the kelly-green door we had painted last summer. It swung open; a surprised Darby stood on the other side. With Malone.

It may have been Sunday, but I had a sneaking suspicion they weren't heading to church. She was still in her hot pink sweat pants and matching hoodie, and he was in his normal Detective Malone uniform.

I had either really good or really bad timing. Depending on which side of the door you were standing on.

"Hey." I smiled, unsure of what to make of the two of them together.

Darby stepped toward me, then abruptly stopped. "I'm sorry. I'm really, really, sorry, Mel," her voice hitched on my name.

My heart plummeted. "What's going on?"

"We're headed downtown," Malone offered.

Oh. My. God. This couldn't be happening. "Is she under arrest?"

"No."

His one word answer didn't eliminate my anxiety, especially when two fat tears slid down Darby's cheeks. She wiped them away with the back of her hand.

"O-kay," I dragged it out waiting for someone to fill in the blanks. No one bothered. "Because of the phone?" I prodded.

Malone looked at me. It was the same look he had at the funeral. "And other things." His voice was void of emotion.

"What other things?" I urged.

His face remained unreadable. Darby's was a mixture of fear and devastation. I wanted to reach for my friend, but Malone's posture clearly communicated that wasn't happening.

"I-I . . ." she shook her head and whispered, "You tell her."

"We found Darby's birth certificate in Mona's safe," Malone said.

I was more confused now than when she'd opened the door. "Why in the world would she have your birth certificate?"

Darby's shoulders sagged in defeat. "Because . . . she's my mother."

I gasped. *Holy crap.*

That was one Texas-sized secret.

Chapter Twenty

After Fluffy and I'd stood there like idiots watching Darby ride off with Malone in his unmarked police car, I'd called Grey. Bless his heart, he agreed to call in a really *big* favor.

I raced home and dropped off the dogs, then quickly changed into jeans, t-shirt and ballet flats (much more appropriate attire for hanging out at a police station). While Malone questioned Darby, I either paced or read the flyers on the bulletin board across from the information desk. I was still reeling from Darby's earth-shattering revelation.

Malone had known about Darby's true parentage at the funeral. Why hadn't he talked to her then?

Darby finally appeared in the hallway. I immediately recognized the prominent man with his expensive black briefcase standing next to her. He'd defended more high-profile defendants, and won, than LA had unemployed actors. Grey had gone above and beyond.

Darby looked worn out and wouldn't hold my gaze for longer than a second or two. I jumped up and hugged her. "Are you okay?" I asked.

She briefly hugged me back. "Yes."

Her reddened nose and puffy eyes tore my heart. "Can you leave?"

She nodded. Before Malone could stop us, we bolted. We drove to the Koffee Klatch, shrouded in heavy silence. I made Darby wait in the Jeep while I ran inside and ordered our usual—to go. Once back in the Jeep, I handed the drinks to Darby and drove directly to my place.

Both dogs greeted us as we walked inside. Missy, wagging, jumping and drooling. Fluffy, sniffing, observing and dismissing.

I tossed them a couple of treats, then we all sat on the couch. The dogs settled between us, not to be denied human contact. Funny how animals just know when we need them the most.

Fluffy sniffed Darby's coffee, who was completely unaware of the hairy beggar at her side.

"Why didn't you tell me?" Oh, geeze. Even I could hear the betrayal and accusation in my voice.

Darby averted her eyes and clutched her cup like a lifeline. "There didn't seem to be a right time."

"Anytime in the last two years would have been better than today."

She shrugged, studying the floor. Fluffy continued to study the coffee. "I didn't know you when I first arrived in Laguna. What was I supposed to say? Oh, by the way, you know that spiteful vindictive lady you despise? She's my biological mother. No worries though, she refuses to acknowledge me."

That would have worked for me. But I could see her point. A revelation like that would be awkward to fit into a conversation.

I got a sudden whiff of Missy's atrocious gas. I waved a pillow in the air and glared at her stinky butt.

"So you came here to be close to Mona?" I asked.

Darby sighed. Her deep breath could have been a struggle for bulldog-fart-free-air, but it was probably because she was about to bare her soul.

"Since I was six-years-old I've known my biological mother abandoned me because I was a mistake."

"That's not true."

Darby shook her head sadly as if erasing years of hurtful memories. "You can't change the truth. To Mona I was a mistake. She left us, me and my dad, when I was a couple of months old. On my twelfth birthday, I secretly started looking for her. She wasn't difficult to find. When my dad found out, he made me promise I wouldn't approach her until I was out of college."

"So you moved here, and then what? Showed up on her doorstep like a long lost relative?" I asked.

She took a drink. Fluffy's long nose followed the cup to Darby's mouth. Darby finally noticed Snob Dog was after her latte and pushed Fluffy's face away.

"I'd manage to get invited to some of the same events or bump into her at the same restaurants."

"You stalked her?" Little Darby had moxie. While I already had respect for my dear friend, I suddenly had a little more.

"One day I worked up the courage to approach her. She looked straight though me."

I couldn't imagine how that had felt. My mama had been the complete opposite. I'd meant so much to her, she'd meddled to the point that she played the horizontal hokey pokey with a Miss America judge.

I set my chai on the end table. Missy took it as an invitation to lay her head in my lap.

"My father had told me that when she left, she never looked back. By the time I realized he was right, I'd met you." A thin smile threatened the corners of her mouth. "You'd convinced me to open the studio. I was making a life for myself here."

I sighed, realizing the depth of the conflict eating at her soul. "But you were holding out for her to come to her senses."

"Stupid, huh?"

A sliver of misguided hope clouded her dark eyes. Her pale skin hung on her cheek bones. She'd never appeared as fragile or naive than this moment.

I reached over the dogs and squeezed her hand. "Not at all."

She cleared her throat and pulled her hand back. "Since I'm spilling all my secrets, I didn't call Mona about the leash."

"I know. You're a terrible liar." This horrible ache must be what Grey had felt when he'd confronted me about Mona's phone.

I waited for Darby to continue, but she sat there unsure and embarrassed. Fluffy readjusted, shoving Darby toward the end of the couch.

"Knock it off, you couch hog. You're not even supposed to be up here," I said. Fluffy didn't acknowledge me. Instead, she rested her head on Darby's leg. Suck up.

"Why *did* you call Mona?"

She picked at the side of her coffee cup, then absently stroked Fluffy's head. "I don't know. I'd had enough of her bullying. I felt responsible for her. Then Jo made a derogatory comment during the shoot. I snapped."

"What did Jo say?"

"It doesn't matter."

I had a feeling it did. "So you called Mona to . . . what?"

"To tell her to stop punishing you because of me."

My stomach twisted in jolt of culpability. "Lord Almighty. That didn't have anything to do with you."

"It doesn't matter. She never answered."

Mona was either already dead or had screened her calls. Darby still looked worried. I had a bad feeling her story was about to get worse.

"Did you leave a message?" I asked.

She looked away.

"What did you say?"

She took a deep breath, then said in a rush, "You're a mean and ugly person, and if you don't stop bullying people, one day someone is going to smash some sense into you."

The reality of the situation hit me. "Oh. My. Word. I delivered you to the police on a gold platter."

"You didn't know."

"Were you really at home that night?"

She nodded franticly. "I swear. My neighbor backed me up. She saw my car in the driveway all night."

Even I knew that wasn't a solid alibi. "Once the police check with the security guard, and he confirms he didn't let you though the gate, they'll have shift their focus," I assured her.

I couldn't continue to sit in the sardine tin any longer. I patted Missy's rump, and she jumped off the couch.

"About that," Darby said, stopping me mid-stretch. "Malone said the guard was AWOL from his station around the time Mona was murdered. Anyone could have come and gone."

"Only if they knew the code . . ." By the guilty look on Darby's face, I had a hunch I wasn't going to like the answer to my next question. "Did *you* know the code?"

She nodded slowly. "I've had a couple of home photo shoots in Mona's neighborhood. Sometimes clients forget to add me to the guest list. They've provided the code so I could let myself in."

I grabbed my empty cup and stomped into the kitchen. "Hells bells, Darby. You didn't tell Malone, did you?"

Darby and the dogs were right on my heels. "I didn't need to. A client ratted me out."

As much as I loved her, I was quickly coming to understand I didn't know Darby. I turned around and crossed my arms. It was time to get down to business. "Why would Mona have you in her cell phone as an emergency contact?"

Missy skidded to a stop directly in front of me. Drool coated her jowls. Fluffy glided past me as if she had somewhere to be, when we all knew she didn't. Darby stood back from all of us, where she was safely out of arms reach. I'm sure it was obvious I wanted to strangle her out of frustration.

"I don't know. It feels like Mona's trying to punish me. But it's not possible, right? She's dead."

I hoisted myself up on the kitchen counter. "Unless you're being framed."

She drifted into the kitchen. "By who? I didn't tell a soul about

Mona. She threatened to ruin my father's business if I told anyone."

Good grief, no wonder Malone was building a case around Darby. "Did you tell Malone she was blackmailing you?"

"Mr. DioGuardi barely let me say my name. Let Grey know I appreciate the referral, but I can't afford his lawyer friend."

I shook my head. "Oh, no. He took your case as a favor to Grey, pro bono."

I jumped off the counter, slid my arm over her shoulder and led her into the living room. The whole situation got me thinking about Caro. Seriously, if she could survive "helping" the police, I would too. She'd dug around on her own and called in Malone once she'd put the pieces together.

Of course, she'd also had to fight off a psycho hit man at gunpoint, but I wasn't about to get myself in that situation. I'd learn from Caro's miscalculations.

Chapter Twenty-One

Darby stayed overnight in the guestroom. (Get this, Fluffy had slept with her. Maybe she could sense they were mourning the same person. Or maybe Fluffy was still trying to steal Darby's coffee.)

Once we'd eaten breakfast and had walked the dogs, I'd convinced Darby to take the day off. There was no telling how much of what had happened last night had made its way into the gossip mill. One more day out of the spotlight seemed like a good idea. And I needed a dog-sitter.

It was a hair down kinda day. Dressed in Burberry Brit skinny jeans and an Armani Collezioni stretch silk top, I pulled on my motorcycle boots—ready to kick some booty. I grabbed my leather jacket from the hall closet and headed to Bow Wow.

I blew through the shop doors by ten-thirty, giving me a solid thirty minutes before I opened. I ran an inventory check on the computer, restocked a few shelves, started the complementary coffee brewing and checked my cell messages.

I had three voicemails, one from Owen, one from Mama, and the last one from Alex, Mona's chauffer. Owen's message was short, simple and swift. Be at his office today at three to discuss Mona's will. Mama's was short and explosive. Call her. Immediately.

Alex's message was puzzling. He was stopping by the boutique to give me something. First, how'd he get my number? Second, what in the world did he have that I'd want? Mona had better not have a secret dog in hiding.

I'd hung the last of the large dog hoodies when my cell rang. Caught up in the task, I yanked the phone out of my jeans back pocket and answered automatically, "Bow Wow Boutique."

"Melinda, are you at work already? Did you talk to Mitchell?" Mama's voice boomed in my ear.

"Yes." I cradled the phone against my shoulder and pulled a stack of pink small dog sweatshirts from the box. I'd already bought two for Missy. On the backside it read, "I Heart Mom."

"And?" Mama asked, out of patience.

I hesitated and grimaced. "He was talkative."

"I knew it. Oh, Melinda." She sounded frantic. "I've left message after message for him for two days. He hasn't returned a single call."

I picked up the empty box and carried it to the counter. "Short of flying to Vegas, Mama, what do you want me to do?"

"Call his friends. Call his boss. Find him."

Why she couldn't do any of that was beyond me. Mitch was fine. He was probably doing what I typically did when she called, ignoring her. On the other hand, if there really was an emergency, and I blew off my brother because our mama was a drama queen, I'd never forgive myself.

"I'll see what I can do." I hung up before I changed my mind. I tossed the phone on the counter. Hopefully she'd forgotten the threat of a surprise visit.

How was I supposed to search for a brother who didn't want to be found while clearing Darby's name? And I still hadn't dealt with Tova and her frivolous lawsuit.

Within minutes of opening Bow Wow for business, a distinguished older gentleman wandered inside. He was of average height and average build. His receding hairline framed a familiar face I was having a hard time placing.

"Hello, Ms. Langston." His salt and pepper moustache smiled.

It was Mona's driver, Alex. His khaki pants, buttoned-down shirt and tweed sports coat threw me. Normally, he wore all black, including a cute little driver's cap.

"Hi, Alex." I met him in front of the dog bowls and treat jars. He held out a strong hand, which I quickly accepted.

"How are you?" he asked.

"Trying to understand Mona's dog. Do you have any advice?"

"Unfortunately, no suggestions. I would consider it a favor if you'd allow me to take her for a ride from time to time. She so enjoyed being chauffeured around town. Of course, you are welcome, too."

"I appreciate the offer, but I'll pass. Fluffy, on the other hand, is yours anytime you want. If you'd like to stop by for a visit today, she's at my place, with Darby."

I motioned for him to follow me to the coffee bar. "Coffee? Tea?" I offered. Southern hospitality was hard to deny.

"Coffee. Black. I heard about Ms. Darby. It's true then?" His steady voice wasn't judgmental, more that he was verifying a rumor.

I poured a mug of coffee and handed it to him. "It's true," I said. "There's proof."

He nodded, but there was something in his eyes that made me a little uneasy.

"The birth certificate," he said.

"Did you know about it?"

"Not at all. Ms. Michaels was a private person. One did not cross the line between employee and employer."

"I see."

I filled my mug with hot water and tossed in a lemon. "Were you with Mona the day she died?" I asked, trying to put my finger on why the alarm bells were ringing in my head.

He sipped his coffee. "Unfortunately, Monday was my day off. I was playing the ponies with friends in Los Alamitos."

"Did you win?"

"A couple hundred." He flashed a self-conscious smile.

The Los Alamitos Race Track was about thirty-five miles northeast of Laguna. Depending on traffic and time of day, the drive was approximately forty-five minutes to an hour.

That wasn't enough time to whack Mona and still make it to the track without being missed. It was doubtful Alex would find his name on my suspect list. Time for a new line of questions.

I know, I know. I promised Malone I'd stay out of his investigation. At the time I gave him my word, I had no intention of getting involved. But that was before Darby was suspect numero uno. I knew in my heart she was innocent. If I didn't find real evidence to point Malone in a different direction, my best friend was about to find herself arrested.

So I did what I do best. I jumped in with both feet, eyes wide open.

"Do you know who might have wanted to hurt Mona?"

He shook his head. "The police questioned me. I'm afraid I didn't have much to tell them."

"What did you tell them?" I asked.

"Ms. Michaels and her ex exchanged words the week she died. Subsequently, she avoided his calls. Now that I've had time to reflect, she was acting quite peculiar really."

"How's that?" I leaned closer, practically begging for anything that might clear Darby.

"She began to spend a significant amount of time away from the house. Upon occasion, she'd asked me to drive without a specific destination."

"Come on now. You went for a joy ride around Laguna?" Please, this wasn't my first rodeo. You couldn't waste more than thirty minutes driving around town.

"San Diego and LA mostly," he said.

As my Daddy would say, "he was as serious as the business end of a .45." How crazy was Mona? Did she think she was being followed? Was she hiding from someone? Or maybe she was really that shallow and bored, and craved adoration even from perfect strangers.

"You never stopped. She didn't get out? No one got in and drove with you?" I asked.

He shook his head and shrugged his shoulder as if to say he couldn't explain her either. "It was always Ms. Michaels and Fluffy." His forehead wrinkled. "There was this one time, the pet psychic came along."

Now we're talking people. "Did you tell the police?"

"I didn't recall until now," he reminded me.

"When was Jo with you? Where'd you go?"

"I believe it was right before the Fur Ball. We picked up the psychic at her business, then drove to San Clemente. I dropped them off for approximately an hour."

For someone who didn't remember all of this important information until thirty seconds ago, he suddenly seemed to have total recall. "Where did you take them?"

"I don't recollect."

I spoke too soon. "Please try, Alex. It could be important. Where did you go?"

His intelligent brown eyes clouded with disappointment. "I'm sorry, Ms. Langston. I truly don't remember. I do keep a log at the garage. If you really think it's important, I can look up the information and get back to you."

"Please do. Did you hear their conversation?"

He shifted his weight. "You understand, part of my job is to *not* hear what my employer says."

This is what I was picking up on. He didn't want to seem disloyal, but he'd sought me out for a reason. "Sometimes you can't help it. Maybe what you accidentally overheard could help find her killer."

His lips thinned, and he turned a wee bit pompous. "I signed a confidentiality agreement. I should not have shared what I have."

He was making me crazy with his back and forth. "Normally, I'd agree. But your boss is dead. She was murdered. I'm sure she'd rather you help find her killer than to keep quiet because of some standard contract every employee in southern California signs."

He cleared his throat. "The psychic told Mona Fluffy didn't like to wear the crown."

That was it? That's what had him twisted in knots like a scared virgin on her wedding night?

That wasn't a big dark secret, which once revealed would save Darby. Well, hells bells. "Trust me, she likes the crown." Sarcasm dripped from each word.

Even I had liked the crowns. At least in the beginning. But then I realized the crowns didn't belong to me. They belonged to my mama. And my Aunt Kat. But never me—the one who'd strutted her stuff across the stage like a 4-H calf at the Texas State Fair.

"Was Mona upset? Mad? Did she believe her?" Did she laugh in Jo's face? Because I sure the heck would have.

A crooked smile tilted the edge of his mouth, and his eyes softened. "I believe her exact words were, 'Don't be a stupid cow.'"

I laughed. Now that sounded like Mona. He must have misinterpreted my amusement.

"Mrs. Michaels didn't have a lot of friends," Alex explained needlessly. "Her personality was . . . difficult."

Difficult. He was endearing, protecting Mona's ruthless reputation. "You're very diplomatic. What was Jo's reaction?"

He tugged at his collar. "They talked quietly most of the time, but I could tell she was upset."

He was downplaying the interaction between them. I set my mug on the coffee bar and closed the space between us, hoping I was instilling confidence. "How upset?"

"She said, 'To me you're dead. I've already said my good-byes.'" He recited the words as if he were auditioning for a Shakespearean play.

Jo did it. Jo killed Mona. I knew it. *I knew it.*

I wanted to jump up and down and clap my hands like a goon. If I'd been alone, I'd have line danced from one end of the store to the other.

I gripped his arm. "Thank you, Alex."

"It would be," he cleared his throat and looked around the empty shop, "inconvenient if it got out that I told you this."

"I understand. I won't say anything unless I have to. But I can't let an innocent person be accused of a crime she didn't commit."

"Of course not. Well, I won't keep you any longer. I came by to give you this." He pulled a small electronic device from his sports coat pocket and held it in the palm of his hand.

"What the heck is it?" I asked, looking it over.

"Fluffy's digital video camera. It attaches to her leather collar."

"She wore this?"

"Upon occasion."

"You're kidding me? How does it work?" I could sell a ton of pet video cameras. A day in the life of your pet would be an instant best seller.

Alex gave me a crash course on the FAQs. It attached to the collar with a special clip on the backside. The rechargeable battery lasted approximately five hours. It recharged and downloaded the recording with a USB cable attached to a computer.

"I found it under the backseat on the passenger side. It must have fallen out of Ms. Michaels purse," he explained.

It was possible the camera may have recorded something important. Determination exploded in my chest. I wanted to close the shop, go home and watch it.

I knew she couldn't have recorded the murder, but maybe she had somehow recorded evidence. What if she'd recorded that last conversation between her and Jo? What if that was already downloaded on her computer? Excitement bubbled with each possibility.

I had to get back to Mona's.

"Please don't let Mr. Michael's know that I gave this to you," Alex asked.

"Sure. Whatever you say," I answered absently before it registered what he'd said. I looked up and asked, "What? Why?"

"He wanted it, but Mrs. Michaels refused to give it to him."

Mona could have refused to hand it over because she was mean and nasty. But that didn't explain why Cliff wanted it.

Before I could ask more questions, the shop door swung open, and television teen star Shar Summers waltzed inside, her Chinese Crested, Babycakes, nestled in the crook of her arm. As God is my witness, Babycakes was one ugly dog. Shar, on the other hand, was adorable. They were both so tiny they could be mistaken for keychain charms.

Pooch and human were decked out in hot pink. Hairless by breed, the pup was wrapped in a pink "fur" coat, which perfectly matched Shar's faux fur vest. They were also wearing black Uggs, Babycakes sporting the doggie kind.

Only the actress wore pink leggings, apparently that was the imaginary line Shar didn't cross—pants for her dog. Go figure.

I caught Alex's horrified look before he recovered and molded a neutral expression to his face. A chuckle lodged in my throat.

"Looks like someone threw up a bottle of Pepto-Bismol, and it splashed all over them," I whispered.

"Indeed."

"Excuse me for a moment," I said, and quickly met the cutesy twosome at the counter. "Hey, Shar. I'm glad you could stop in. Are you ready for your trip to Europe?"

Her TV series, *Bibbidi Bobbidi Boo*, about triplets who perform magic, was filming an episode in England. Just for clarification, there weren't triplets, just Shar, playing triplets.

She covered Babycake's ears, one of the few parts on his miniature body with hair. "Shh. It's a surprise. Baby doesn't know we're taking a widdle twip."

I cringed at her baby talk. I never understood why people insisted on talking down to their baby, let alone their animal. Especially people with small dogs.

I lowered my voice, "I have your special order in the office. I'll grab it."

I wanted to get back to Alex as quickly as I could. I hurried to the storage area and immediately found the plush white box containing the $35,000 doggles Shar had commissioned. (No, that's not a typo. Let me spell it out—thirty-five thousand dollars. For sunglasses. For a dog. *Hello!*)

I hadn't been gone for more than two minutes, but that was enough time for Alex to escape my questions. Dang.

I set the box on the counter and slid it to Shar. "Here you go."

"I'm not sure I should open it in front her." She pushed out her bottom lip and looked at me expectantly.

As if I'd ever let myself be manipulated by pouting. Sheesh. There was no way I'd hold that dog. Last I'd heard she'd not only bitten Caro, but she'd bitten Detective Malone, too.

Thinking about Malone made me think about Mona, which made me think about how often Cliff's name popped up. He could have killed Mona. He had motive and opportunity. And it would have been easy for him to get into the gated community without drawing attention.

Then there was Jo. Like Darby, Jo couldn't have gotten into the neighborhood without the guard letting her though or without using the access code. Did Jo have other clients in the neighborhood? Could they have given her the access code?

"Well?" Shar asked, pulling me out of my mental-sleuthing.

It was time to get rid of Bibbidi-Bobbidi-Two so I could bop over to Mona's and find her computer. "How about, I open the box and hold it above Baby's head?"

She looked lovingly at her pooch, then nodded. "I guess so."

I pried open the box, showcasing rimless sunglasses with diamonds in the shape of hearts on the pink lenses. I held it just above Babycakes' head like I said I would.

A soft growl started at the back of her throat (uh, the baby dog, not the baby girl). I remained calm, but I had zero confidence teenage blondie could handle her itty bitty doggie.

"Are you sure that's the right shade of pink?" Shar asked.

Baby's almond eyes stared me down. "Positive. Pink Bubble Gum." I closed the box and moved out the line of biting.

Shar whipped out her pink Coach wallet and handed me her black credit card. I rang up the doggles, then handed the receipt and bag to Shar.

"I put a couple of sweet potato treats in the bag."

"Thanks, Mel."

I followed them to the door, locking it as soon as their baby feet hit the sidewalk. I quickly hung the closed sign before more business wandered inside. I was a woman on a mission. I'd clear Darby's name and, in the process, find out who hated Mona so much they killed her.

Chapter Twenty-Two

The sun had quickly burned off the morning clouds. It was noon, and the day promised to be full of sunshine and hope. I headed to Mona's without calling, fingers crossed Camilla would be apron deep in recording Mona's possessions. By now the security guard didn't bother to stop me and passed me through. At some point I'd been promoted to resident status.

Is that what had happened the night Mona had died? Had he waved through a murderer? Or did they live in the community? I made a mental note to talk to the guard on my way out.

I parked in Mona's circular driveway. I marched up to the door, and knocked as I opened it.

"Camilla? It's Melinda. Are you here?" I yelled out, closing the door behind me.

She came rushing downstairs. "Why you here? Fluffy OK?"

Camilla looked really comfortable hanging out in Mona's house in her black t-shirt and designer jeans. *Uh, hello?* Since when did housekeepers wear two hundred dollar jeans?

Instead of the "butler did it," could it be the housekeeper did it?

"She's fine." It probably wasn't smart to let on I suddenly considered her a possible suspect. "Did you hear about the will?"

"Si, I got phone call."

The meeting at Owen Quinn's was in three hours. I needed to hurry this up. I peered over Camilla's shoulder searching for what would be a logical office for Mona.

She looked over her shoulder too. "What?"

"So, you'll be there? At the meeting."

She shook her head. "No. My sister's leaving town. I taking her to airport."

"She can't take a taxi?" If I was broke and thought I might be on the receiving end of a windfall of cash, my sister would be finding her own way to the airport. Okay, not really. But if Camilla didn't attend the meeting, how would I know for sure if she was guilty or innocent?

"Taxi?" she asked confused.

"You're not leaving town, too, are you?"

She laughed lightly, wiping her hands on her jeans. "No, no. I take my sister to the airport. She's flying to Kansas."

"Camilla, can I ask you a question?"

"Of course, Miz Melinda. Come with me."

I followed Camilla to the sunroom and kept my eye out for an office. I positioned myself onto the settee across from her. "Did you know Darby Beckett was Mona's daughter?" I asked.

She shook her head, her brows furrowed in concern. "No. It was big surprise. Do you think there are more children?" She asked the last part in a whisper.

Good grief. I hadn't thought about that possibility.

I studied Mona's former housekeeper with a critical eye. Was she curious, or was she more devious than I'd given her credit for? Maybe she thought if there were more offspring she'd get a smaller slice of the money pie.

"I doubt it," I said. "Did Mona and Cliff argue last week about Fluffy?"

She shook her head automatically. "No."

"No, you don't know, or no they didn't?"

"No argument."

"Are you sure? Think carefully. Did Cliff stop by unannounced or call?"

She scowled. "No. He never come here. Once she kicked him out," she jerked her thumb over her shoulder, "he never be back."

She was lying. Kate, from the dog park, had been very clear—Cliff had been here, and they'd fought. Unless Kate was lying. Or maybe she didn't know what Cliff looked like and just assumed the man Mona had argued with was Cliff.

But what other man would Mona have fought with? Alex?

Was Alex lying?

What if they were all lying?

I rubbed my temples. I was giving myself a headache. I leaned in closer. "You're certain, Cliff was never here?"

She shifted her weight, mirroring my posture. She stared at me, freakishly unblinking. "Si."

Camilla was lying. Was she hiding behind the same confidentiality agreement as Alex? Could she be protecting Mona? Or herself? Where was Camilla the night Mona had died?

"The police think Darby may have had something to do with Mona's death," I said, trying to work in a way to ask for an alibi for the night of the murder.

"She killed Miz Mona?" She crossed herself and looked to the ceiling.

I caught myself wanting to look at the ceiling, too. "No. That's why I'm here. She cared about Mona."

"She loved Miz Mona?" Skepticism tinged her question.

"I wouldn't go that far, but she did care."

She considered my words before she spoke. "Miz Mona was mad about a letter from her lawyer," she offered.

"From Owen Quinn? Do you know what it was about?"

"I don't snoop," she said, full of indignation.

I'm sure if she did know, she'd never tell. If word got out that she was into Mona's business, Camilla wouldn't find another job within five hundred miles of the OC.

"I didn't mean to imply that you do. Did," I corrected myself. "I thought Mona might have confided in you."

"No, no, no. She not like me."

Well, I wasn't expecting that. I wanted to ask outright if she'd killed her, but my gut told me it wasn't her. If so, she'd have thrown Darby under the bus without hesitation. But that didn't explain why she lied about Cliff.

"I'm just curious, where were you when Fluffy and I found Mona? I called out your name. I expected you to pop out of a room any moment."

She shook her head. "I not live here. Monday night my day off. All staff have Monday night off. Miz Mona liked to be alone."

"Do you know Kate?"

"The dog walker? Of course."

"When was the last time Kate walked Fluffy?"

"The day of the Fur Ball," she answered automatically.

Kate was telling the truth. "I met her at the Bark Park. She said Cliff was here that day, and he and Mona argued."

Camilla didn't say anything. She pushed her lips together, telling me they were sealed. She fought her own silent war.

I reached out and patted her knee. "You can tell me. Mona isn't here to punish you for telling the truth."

Out of nowhere, the water works spewed like a geyser. Fat salty tears spilled out of her eyes and splashed onto us both. Holy cow.

"I lied," she wailed. "Mr. Michaels was here. He come a lot. They argue about the other Mr. Michaels. Miz Michaels make me promise not to talk about it."

She pulled out a wadded used tissue from her pocket and eventually found a section to blow her nose. And blow her nose. And then blow it one more time. Eew.

"The other Mr. Michaels? Cliff has a brother?" I guessed.

"Si. Mr. Ted."

"Do you have a picture of Ted?" I had no idea what he looked like.

"Si." She got up, still sniffling, and rummaged through the antique buffet table's drawers. She pulled out a frame that had been shoved into the back and handed it to me, then returned to her seat.

It was a candid picture of Cliff and the man who'd attended the funeral with him. "Why were they arguing about him?"

"I don't snoop in Miz Mona's business." She said pointedly, her tears drying up as quickly as they'd started.

Yeah, yeah. She was talking about me. "You don't have to stick your nose into someone business to overhear an argument. People yell when they fight."

Apparently, that was all the prodding she needed to spill her guts. "Mr. Michaels, Cliff, wanted Miz Mona to give his brother money. He says Mr. Michaels, Ted, owed a bad man lots of money. He said Miz Mona better do what he said or she'd be sorry."

Foreboding shimmied down my back. "Did you hear how much money he owed or to who?"

She shredded her tissues into confetti and said quietly, "I heard the name. Tommy 'Batty' Coppola." She crossed her herself and whispered to the ceiling again.

Holy Batman.

If I believed crossing myself would protect me, I'd do it, too. Ted Michaels owed money to the mob. That changed everything.

Tommy's nickname was "Batty." Not because he was crazy, although he was, but because he was never without his bat. The bat he used to break knee caps, hands or heads. Whatever he felt like at the moment.

Camilla wasn't keeping mum because of Mona, but for her own protection. It was all coming together. I handed the picture back.

"What are you going to do now? Do you have plans?" Like hot footing it to Brazil?

She shook her head. "I don't have new job yet. Do you need

housekeeper?" A hopeful smile landed on her round face.

"No, thanks. I'm good." I hopped up and motioned toward the hall. "Do you mind if I look through Mona's stuff?"

"*La policia* take most of it."

She led me to what I would call the library. Or office. The built-in bookcases and desk were a dead giveaway. Most of the shelves were empty. Half packed boxes haphazardly littered the room along with files and loose papers.

"Does she have a computer?" I asked.

"*Si.* They take it."

Of course they did. And whatever Fluffy's home camera may have recorded.

"Does Fluffy ever wear a different collar than the one she's wearing now?"

Camilla stopped fidgeting and looked at me uneasily. "I pack all her belongings. It's not my fault you not take everything."

"I'm not blaming you for anything. Stop talking crazy. Where's the stuff I left here?"

"Mr. Quinn take care of it. I don't steal." She lifted her chin defiantly.

Okay. Someone had obviously accused Camilla of thievery. "Who accused you of stealing?"

She pitched forward, her face scrunched up in disgust. "Miz Edwards accused me of hiding Miz Mona's important papers. I didn't do it."

"Tricia was here?"

"Si, yesterday. I don't like her."

That made two of us. "I'm sure the police confiscated whatever it is she's looking for. Don't worry about Tricia. She's as empty as the designer handbags tucked in the back of her closet. Back to Fluffy. Have you ever seen her wearing this?" I pulled the dog video recorder from the inside pocket of my leather jacket.

Camilla crossed herself at warp speed and backed up until she'd pressed herself flat against the wall with a bang. "Take it away," she yelled.

Shocked at her reaction, I immediately shoved it back in my pocket. "It's just a pet recorder."

Mona's housekeeper was visibly shaken. "Mr. Michaels come here for that. Miz Mona refuse to give it to him. He scream at her. She scream at him. She called it her *seguro*." Words rushed out of her mouth like an amateur hip hop rapper trying to make a quick buck.

"What's *seguro*?"

"Insurance." Her accent thick on the single word. She crossed herself once more for good measure, then fled from the room.

Hells bells. I had to see what was on Fluffy's digital video camera.

Chapter Twenty-Three

I had one hour 'til the reading of the will. I headed back to Bow Wow with more questions than answers. When I'd arrived at Mona's, I'd leaned toward Jo as the killer. Now I believed it was Cliff.

I unlocked the shop door. Lately, the boutique was closed more than it was open. I turned on the laptop in my office and rummaged through the desk drawers for a USB cable. I couldn't find one.

Within minutes of my return, Bow Wow was full of customers. I abandoned my search and tended to business. I sold a few pounds of Bowser Treats, a handful of doggie sweaters and a tiara. The whole time I was thinking about the video camera tucked in my jacket pocket.

I'd also overheard gossip.

Not that anyone was trying to keep it a secret. Most of the talk was inaccurate but close enough to the truth that if I hadn't been at the funeral, I might have believed it myself.

Instead of Tricia and Jo fighting in the bathroom, they'd fought in the vestibule. And instead of Cliff being accosted in the parking lot by some random stranger, he'd been arrested by Malone.

After talking to Camilla, I was pretty sure his visitor wasn't random or a stranger, but someone from the mob. He was lucky he'd gotten out of there alive. If Detective Malone hadn't followed Cliff to his car, Cliff would have been batting practice.

Were the police aware of Cliff's side venture? It was possible Mona's death had been a mob hit. What if Batty had one of his boys knock her off to scare Cliff? It was time to call Malone. Lord, I dreaded that conversation.

The last customer walked out the door as Tricia breezed inside with a humongous Michael Kors tote. And a cloud of Mona's signature perfume.

"Make it quick. I have somewhere to be in thirty minutes."

"We had a meeting this afternoon. You were closed." She was all business in her Prada suit as she headed straight for the counter where I was standing.

"With Mona dead that appointment was canceled."

She smoothed the skirt of her dress. "Now it's uncanceled."

"You can't uncancel an appointment." Uncancel wasn't even a word. "This isn't a good idea."

"What? Meeting today?"

"Everything. You, me. I'm not interested."

"You will not kick me to the curb because Mona's dead. She wouldn't approve." Tricia flipped her blond hair off her shoulder and tried her version of a Mona glare. She had a long way to go before she'd achieve Mona's level of bored disdain.

"I couldn't give a flying fig for what Mona would or wouldn't approve. If you remember, I didn't want to sell your dog line in the first place. How can I market a clothing line by someone who hates dogs?"

"I don't hate dogs," she huffed, eyes lids fluttering in protest. "I certainly don't hate Fluffy."

Who was she kidding? She'd called Fluffy a beast on more than one occasion. If Tricia had a sudden love-fest for Snob Dog, it was because she was worth millions.

As she stood rooted in front of me with her superior attitude, I remembered something Camilla had said. "Speaking of Mona, what were you looking for at her place yesterday?"

Tricia dropped her bag on the counter. "You've spoken to Camilla." She spread two extravagant dog dresses in front of me. "She's a hysterical mess. I don't trust her for a minute."

I picked up the lavender ballerina dress. It was absolutely adorable. Damn. "So you accused her of stealing?"

Her head snapped up, eyes narrowed. "Yes."

"What do you think she took?"

"The signed contact between Mona and me."

That didn't make any sense. "Shouldn't you have your own copy?"

She blinked a couple of times, surprise fighting her Botoxed forehead. "I misplaced it. I'd asked Mona for a copy, and she said she'd make me one. I never got it. You've obviously snooped through Mona's belongings, maybe you saw it."

I didn't believe her for a doggone minute. "I'm sure either the police or Owen have Mona's legal documents." I had no idea what I was saying. I was making stuff up as I went along. I didn't even know if her so called contract even existed.

My gut said Tricia was hiding something, and I wanted to know what. I picked up the second dress, a cute denim with pink flowers and crystals, perfect for Shar's Babycakes. It dawned on me Tricia had been using Mona to get her business off the ground. Without her, Tricia would have to find a new investor.

"Did Mona owe you money?" I asked.

She snatched the dog dress from my hands. "What are you talking about?"

"Most contracts involve money changing hands. You're looking for the contract, minutes before the reading of the will."

Tricia packed away her samples haphazardly. "You do realize it's not a reading like you see on TV? Owen will give you a copy of the paperwork, you'll sign a release, and that will be the end of it."

I didn't know that. I had imagined everyone sitting around while Owen read off who was getting what and who wasn't getting what they thought they deserved. Apparently, it wasn't so dramatic. I watched Tricia with renewed interest. How many will readings had she been to that she was so well versed in the procedures?

"Thanks for the heads up. Your samples are charming. What were you and Jo arguing about at the funeral?"

Her shrewd brown eyes turned on me. "That's none of your business."

"It's not, but you should tell me. I don't trust Jo, and I can't believe for a minute Mona actually believed Jo could predict the future."

"You're wrong. Mona did believe. And it turned out she was right."

At some point Tricia had to stop living in the land of denial. "Did you ever stop to think maybe Jo had something to do with Mona's death?"

"That's ridiculous. If anything, Cliff and his brother are responsible for Mona's death. They just wanted her money."

Hello, pot. Was she listening to herself? She wasn't any different than Cliff and his brother. She wanted Mona's money, too, although she probably wasn't dumb enough to borrow money from the mob.

"Cliff constantly harassed her for cash for himself and Ted."

I nodded. "Batty."

"So you've heard."

I wasn't about to throw Camilla under the bus. "Stuff like that gets around. Why would they hook up with the mob?"

She looked at me with a smug smile. "You don't know as much as you think."

"But as Mona's best friend you do." I appealed to her vanity.

"The Michaels brothers like to drink and gamble."

Again, Captain Obvious. Even my Mama knew about Cliff's "vices." "I've never asked you this before, but where were you when Mona was killed?"

Tricia snapped her bag shut. "I've already given a statement to the police. Since you're not the police, I don't have to answer." Contempt oozed off her tongue.

I didn't believe for a minute she was the killer, but her reaction confirmed my earlier gut feeling she was hiding something. "You're right, you don't have to. But since you don't have anything to hide, why wouldn't you?"

"I was on a date."

That wasn't what I thought she'd say. "With who?"

"No one you know. My private life is not open for discussion." A sense of false bravado shrouded poor Tricia. She just didn't have the same tone of contempt as Mona.

She was *so* hiding something.

Because it's Laguna, and we're a stone's throw from LA, I have to admit, my first thought was she was dating a married man. Why else would she want to keep him a secret? The name of the game in her social circle was to be seen with someone higher on the social ladder than yourself.

What if Mona knew who Tricia was dating, and it was a scandal waiting to break? Maybe that's what Tricia was really looking for. Not a contract, but proof of her private life.

Like pictures she didn't want anyone else to see.

If someone had told me I'd feel sorry for Mona, I'd have thought they were crazy. But with each day I was learning she was one of those unfortunate people who wouldn't know if someone was her friend or if they saw her as nothing more than a cash cow.

It had to be a miserable existence.

Tricia wanted Mona for her name and money. That wasn't a motive for murder. With Mona dead, Tricia didn't have a backer. Cliff and his brother wanted Mona to pay off their gambling debts. If she was dead, she couldn't cough up the cash. It seemed they didn't have a motive either.

Unless Mona had cut off Cliff's money, so he killed her out of anger. Maybe that's what Kate had heard them arguing about? What if Mona hadn't changed her will right away, and Cliff thought she was worth more dead than alive? That was certainly a motive for whacking his rich ex-wife.

After further thought, I'd given up on the mob hit. Mona was killed with a trophy, not a bat. She had to have been killed in of a moment of passion. If it had been planned, the killer would have brought a weapon.

That left Jo. Jo wanted Mona for . . . I hadn't figured that part out. What did Jo want? To make a name for herself? If Mona Michaels was a believer, wouldn't that draw a larger client base? But Jo had stupidly predicted Mona's death. So if Mona didn't die, people would believe she was a fake.

I was missing something. Jo needed Mona alive *and* dead. Unless Jo was in cahoots with Tricia. Or Cliff. Now that would be something. I needed to talk to Jo. But first, I was about to find out the biggest motive of all.

Mona's will.

Chapter Twenty-Four

It was a gathering of the crazy people.

"This-isn't-how-we-typically-handle-estate-disbursements-but-these-are-rather-unusual-circumstances," Owen Quinn talked at warp-speed. He looked like a miniature action figure sitting behind his chunky cherry wood desk.

There were four of us: Tricia, Alex, myself, and the surprise guest of the afternoon—Cliff. We were seated in Owen's corner office with an ocean view. Our swivel leather chairs formed a semicircle around his desk as if it were a campfire. Instead of singing *Boom Chicka Boom*, we waited to hear if our lives were going to be enriched by Mona's wealth.

Boy, were we in for a rude awakening.

"Each of you is named in Mona's will." Owen stood. At least I think he did; he was vertically challenged, which made it difficult to know for certain. He passed everyone a handful of papers with red "sign here" tabs sticking out the right side. So far Tricia's description of the meeting was dead on.

He paced behind his desk. "Now, as you can see, Ms. Michaels left all of you something—"

"It says she left me her cars."

That was Alex. He'd acted as if we barely knew each other. I played along for now.

"The housekeeper didn't bother to show. Does she get to keep the money?"

That was Cliff. The cad.

"I don't see Melinda's name. Why is she here?"

I'm sure I don't have to tell you, that was Tricia.

"Melinda was named Fluffy's guardian," Owen explained.

"She really gets Fluffy?" Tricia whined, spinning her chair in my direction.

"Very well played, indeed." Alex muttered under his breath. He seemed to approve of my guardianship. Maybe he'd trade me, the cars for the dog.

"I should get Fluffy," Cliff bellowed.

"Mona left the ARL three million dollars?" Tricia complained.

Don Furry would be ecstatic to learn he'd get his donation after all.

"Please don't get caught up in what Mona left you. Or didn't leave you. Okay? The reason for this meeting is to inform all of you she filed for bankruptcy a month ago. She had no assets. Only bills." Owen's oversized eyebrows danced with each word, his impatience with us evident.

"What are you saying?" Tricia asked, a hint of panic in her voice.

"Mona's broke," Owen said.

The room erupted into immediate chaos. Chairs oscillated like fans as everyone shouted simultaneously.

Bummer. Don wasn't going to get his money.

"You've got to be kidding."

"There must be some mistake."

"Impossible. I would have known."

"Do the police know about Mona's, ah, financial situation?" I asked.

Owen nodded. "Yes."

And the questions continued. *She was broke? How could Mona have declared bankruptcy and no one knew? What do you mean I don't get anything?*

"It says right here I'm supposed to get five hundred thousand dollars. I can read," Tricia yelled.

Alex looked confused. "So I don't get the cars?"

Owen nodded. "The estate must be liquidated in order to pay off her debt and taxes. That's happening now. Think of it as a high end tag sale. Unfortunately, there won't be enough assets to cover the amount owed."

I think Owen Quinn talked so fast because he wanted all the crazy people out of his office.

"What about Fluffy? Does she have to be liquidated too?" I asked. A guardian had to try.

"No, no, no. Fluffy's not a part of the estate. She has her own money."

"Yet she," Tricia's boney finger pointed toward me, "gets a million dollars? And that *Darby* gets two million dollars?" Her voice took on a shrill tone with each word.

Owen sighed and rubbed his tired brown eyes. "Those are insurance policies and aren't tied to the estate. Ms. Becket is the beneficiary of one, and Fluffy is the beneficiary of the other."

Darby wasn't present. Because she didn't know about the meeting or chose to stay away, I had no idea. For whatever reason, it was for the best. She'd have been mugged before she ever left the room.

"And the dog?" Cliff asked, dollar signs flashing in his eyes, temper rising.

"The dog belongs to Melinda," Owen reminded him.

"Along with her money?" he bit out.

At least she didn't cut you out of the will. I was more than surprised Mona had left him her art collection. I also found it curious he was concerned about the money and not if he'd retained his visitation rights now that I was Fluffy's guardian. But I kept my mouth shut and waited for Owen to explain.

Mona's lawyer sat in his chair and propped his elbows on the desk. "The money belongs to Fluffy, not Melinda. Melinda is the controller of the money, which is in a separate trust Mona had set up years ago. The trust is very specific on how the money is to be used."

I quickly scanned the papers Owen had handed me. Grooming, food, bodyguard and caretaker. Wow, I got paid. Then I saw the amount and realized why Cliff was shooting me a death glare. Ninety grand a year. Fluffy's bodyguard got one hundred and twenty thousand.

"If there are no more questions," Owen stood, excusing us from his office.

I looked up from the legal documents I'd been studying. It looked like we had a missing person on our hands.

"Who's Fluffy's bodyguard?"

Chapter Twenty-Five

Good news! There wasn't a missing person because Fluffy didn't have a bodyguard. Bad news. It was my responsibility to hire one.

I knew the perfect person for the job. I also knew there was no way on God's green earth I'd convince Grey to agree. I put that action item on the back burner in favor of a different item that needed my attention. Tova Randall.

While everyone had argued and fought over what money they weren't getting, I'd thought about Tova and the money she wanted, but I wouldn't give her. Both Owen and Nigel (the family lawyer) had separately recommended that I settle of out court. It was a nuisance suit and would cost more to fight than to just pay her off. As much as I didn't want to do it, I was beginning to agree.

Tova Randall needed to go away.

Which is how I found myself pulling up to Tova's pad just before five o'clock. Her place was exactly what you'd imagine thirteen million dollars would buy. Huge, extravagant, and the best view of the Pacific Ocean you'd ever seen, except there were zero luscious flowers in her front yard. A handful of anorexic trees, some bushy ferns and wild grass, but no color.

I knocked on Tova's oversized double-doors, not exactly sure of what to say, but I knew what I needed to do. The right door swung open.

Tova's expression went from surprise, to confusion, to finally suspicion. "What are you doing here?" she asked, hands planted on her bony hips (and they were bony; her velour sweatpants were falling down showing off her lower body).

She stood, legs apart, blocking me from casually entering her home.

"I wanted to talk. Can I come in?"

She didn't budge. "You shouldn't be here."

I sighed. "Fine. We can talk out here."

I got right to the point before she caught a cold. "I've thought about it, and I'm willing to pay the fifteen hundred dollars."

Tova crossed her arms, raising the girls and her top, exposing her bellybutton. "Why now?"

I shoved my hands in my back pockets, biding my time. I knew if I said the wrong thing it was over. "It doesn't matter. Check or cash?"

She tapped her bare foot and studied me. "Are you trying to buy me off?"

Whoa. Who would have thought she'd be so quick to assess the situation accurately? Back-peddle time. "You accosted me at the Fur Ball demanding money. Now that I'm willing to pay, you're accusing me of buying you off?"

"You admit you have fleas?" Her eyebrows rose.

"No." I shifted my weight to one leg. I tried to relax and not grow impatient. "I'm paying you the money."

"You owe me an apology, too."

"Excuse me?" I cocked my head to the side. I had to have heard her wrong.

"You made fun of me in public. Twice. You owe me two apologies." She held up two fingers.

Hello. I can count to two. This was painful. "Tova, I don't think you understand. I just came by to pay you—"

"Check."

Oh, my gosh. She was crazy. Why did I come here? "What?"

"You can write me a check while I call my lawyer." She turned around and started to close the door.

I shoved my foot in the doorway (thank the good Lord for motorcycle boots with Vibram soles), keeping it from slamming in my face. "Hold on. There's no need to involve attorneys."

"Did you think I'd drop the lawsuit?"

"Yes. You wanted me to pay you—"

She pointed her finger in my face. "I want an apology. Public."

What was it with the public apologies? First Mona and now Tova. I leaned back before I followed the urge to swat her finger.

"Look, Tova, that's not going to happen."

"I'm still suing you. Unless you want to apologize and admit you have fleas."

A wave of anger washed over me at my own stupidity. "All I have to do is find one other client who attends Mommy and Doggie Yoga who has fleas, and you'll lose."

"That won't prove anything."

"It will if they've never set foot in Bow Wow. And then your little lawsuit will go down in flames, and you'll wish you would have taken my fifteen hundred dollars. Especially when I sue you for slander."

"You won't find them." She didn't sound convinced.

I removed my foot from the doorway. The determination that had propelled me through the last ten years of my life pounded in my soul. "Wanna bet?"

Tova stumbled backwards at the intensity of my stare. She was about to learn the hard way—win or lose, I never back down from a challenge.

Once I'd left Tova's and had cooled off, I headed for my place looking for Darby. She was gone. So I pointed the Jeep toward Paw Prints. Sure enough, her sparkly blue Fiesta was parked out front.

I went inside and called out for her. I didn't see her right away, but I spotted Snob Dog sprawled out on the couch.

"Seriously, who knew you were such a couch potato?"

Darby appeared, carrying a large letter-sized manila envelope.

"I thought you were hanging out at my place," I said.

"I was, until my attorney called." She dropped the envelope on the coffee table. Her expression strained. "It's official. I'm a person of interest. I'm not supposed to leave town without talking to the police first."

"I thought that only happened on TV?"

The stress of the situation played out on her face. "I guess not. I have a packet of paperwork from my attorney that I'm supposed to read through and fill out."

I opened the envelope and fingered through the papers. Questionnaires, personal information, affidavits—the gravity of the situation made my heart sink.

"Why's the boutique closed?" she asked.

I shoved the paperwork into the envelope and tossed it back on the table. "I just came from Tova's, and before that I was at Owen's. He went over the will with Tricia, Alex, me . . . and Cliff."

Darby's mouth dropped open. "I'm not sure where to start. Why in the world did you go to Tova's? Cliff was at the reading of the will?"

"Tova's was a mistake. I don't want to relive it. The other was a gathering of the moochers. It wasn't really a reading as much as it was to let everyone know Mona was one hundred percent broke, and, even though we were in the will, we get nothing."

"You're in the will? *Cliff's* in the will? Did you just say she was broke?"

I nodded and shoved Fluffy aside so I'd have somewhere to sit too. "Somehow she'd managed to declare bankruptcy without anyone knowing, except for her lawyer. I get Fluffy. Mona left Cliff her art. But because she went bust, he doesn't get it."

Darby drifted to the table and sat. "I don't understand. She hated him more than she hated me."

"The line between love and hate is thinner than we realized. The only people missing from out little faux family gathering were you and Camilla."

"Owen Quinn called while I was with my attorney. He left a voicemail. Apparently, Mona left me some money. He made it sound like it was a substantial amount. Is it true?" Darby couldn't keep the tiny seed of hope out of her question. "Or is it like Cliff's art and gone?"

I watched her carefully, noting her reaction to finding out she was now rolling in the deep end of money.

"She named you as the beneficiary of one of her life insurance policies. Two million dollars. It's all yours. Separate from her estate."

Darby sat transfixed. In an instant, she snapped out of it and jumped up. "There must be some mistake. You misunderstood."

"No mistake," I said softly. Inside I was jumping with excitement for her newfound wealth, but Darby was having a mini-meltdown.

"I don't want it." She started to pace, her voice thin. "I won't accept it. You take it."

"What? No way. You deserve it. Besides, she was broke. The only money left is from her insurance policies."

"I can't. Don't you see? This will only convince Malone I killed Mona."

I hadn't thought about that. For the first time, I was unsure if I should comfort my friend or just let her wear herself out.

"I don't accept it." Darby raised a fist into the air and yelled at the ceiling, "Why did you hate me so much?"

"I don't think you get to decide," I said with a half smile.

She wiped her hands on her skirt and shared a shaky grin of her own. "Yes, I do. I respectfully decline. I choose to remain poor. Let's change the subject. Alex came by and took Fluffy for a ride. She was happy to see him."

I loved her spunk. There was no way I was letting her refuse that inheritance. Mona owed her that much. For now, I followed her lead in subject changing and glanced at Fluffy, who was now stretched out on the rug. "It must have been exhausting, being chauffeured around."

"I hope you don't mind, I told Alex to drop her off here when they were finished. I left Missy at your place. She seemed to enjoy the peace and quiet."

"Don't let her fool you. She's just recharging," I said.

I followed Darby further into the studio and helped her put the props away.

"I saw Tricia leaving Bow Wow. What did she want?"

I quickly filled her in on how Tricia had demanded Fluffy, had practically thrown Cliff under the bus for murder, and had claimed she was on a date the night Mona was murdered. "She completely clammed up when I asked her about Jo. I'm going pay Ms. O'Malley a surprise visit. Maybe she'll tell me what they argued about."

"There's no need. Leave it alone." She tossed a handful of oversized plastic sunglasses into a wicker storage basket.

"What does that mean?" I grabbed a pair of neon green glasses from the basket and slid them on my face. "We've got to find a way to clear your name before Malone arrests you."

Darby rolled her eyes at my attempt to lessen the tension. "My lawyer has hired a private investigator. You need to stay out of it before you get hurt."

I pulled an electric blue boa from the shelf and draped it around Darby's shoulders. "You're watching more television than I am. I can't get hurt by asking questions," I said.

"Yes, you can."

I wrapped a purple boa around my neck and struck a pose. "You think whoever killed Mona will come after me?" I'm sure I looked ridiculous with my clown glasses and boa, but I'd made Darby smile, and that's all I cared about.

"It's possible. You're a dork."

"We are going to clear your name, and you're going to keep that money," I promised.

The front door opened and in sauntered Jo. Speak of the devil. I couldn't believe my luck. Once again, Jo's red hair looked like an untamed beehive from the sixties.

"And it starts right now," I said under my breath.

"Hey, Jo. Missed you at the will reading this afternoon."

She looked at me like I was a Hollywood hooker. I hated to burst her bubble, but she'd be working the opposite corner.

"Hello, Melinda," she replied as if she were bored by my very presence. She turned her attention to Darby. "I came by to pick up my head shots. You said they were on a CD."

Darby yanked off her boa and tossed it in the storage basket. "Sorry, we were just cleaning up. I'll get them." She paused, looking between Jo and me with concern. "Behave," she muttered in my direction.

I slowly removed the glasses. "I guess you and Mona weren't as buddy buddy as you thought."

Jo dropped all pretenses. "What do you want?" Her foghorn voice boomed throughout the studio.

I yanked off the boa and stuffed the props in their proper places, then turned my undivided attention to Jo.

"I left before you and Tricia could finish your argument in the bathroom at the funeral. Fill me in on what I missed." The time for finessing and coddling was over. Besides, it wouldn't take Darby but a few minutes before she was back.

"No." She spun around and marched toward the front of the studio, the soles of her boots squeaking on the cement floor.

I followed. "Let me tell you what I think you argued about. I think Mona decided you were a fraud and was going to out you, but someone killed her first."

She whipped around. "Are you accusing me of murder?"

I'm sure the Lassie tattoo under her sleeve was snarling at me.

I guess I was accusing her of murder. "Did you kill Mona?"

"Absolutely not."

"Her last outgoing phone call was to you."

"How do you know?" She frowned, and for a second I could have sworn fear flashed in her eyes.

Jo was suddenly seeing me in a whole new light. Maybe even as a threat. I'm not sure that was good, but I pushed it out of my mind and continued my questions. "Why did she call you?"

"She wanted to meet."

"Why?"

"I don't know, Melinda. Someone killed her first. Look, you have no idea what you're talking about." She plastered a sneer on her face.

"Then fill me in. I'm all ears. Wait, don't tell me. You had another dream?"

Her body stiffened. "As a matter of fact I did."

"I can't wait to hear about it. Did Fluffy predict another murder?"

"No. I saw Cliff with Tricia."

I was suddenly confused. "What do you mean?"

"Cliff and Tricia were having an affair."

It was as if we were living a soap opera. What was next, Mona was going to reappear alive. Maybe it was all a bad dream?

"Do you have proof?" I asked.

"I don't need proof," she answered coolly.

"You can't convince me Mona believed you just because you say you had a dream."

Darby came rushing out of her office, face flushed and out of breath. "Here you go. Sorry it took so long, I . . ." she looked between us. "What's going on?"

"I was right. Jo has information that might help clear you."

Darby looked skeptical. "Oh?"

"Either you can tell her, or I will. She deserves to know since she's the one the police are trying to pin Mona's murder on," I said.

Jo plucked the CD from Darby's hand. A feline smile spread across her mouth. "She already knows," she purred, (as well as a foghorn could) and scampered out of the studio.

I was getting used to the feeling of being blindsided all too well. Once again, Darby had some explaining to do.

Chapter Twenty-Six

It was hard to trust Darby when she kept more secrets than Grey. At least Grey had a legitimate reason. The same could not be said for Darby.

Once Jo had ambushed me with her newest Cliff factoid, there was no stopping me from my own field trip. Darby, still convinced I could somehow be harmed, volunteered to be my wing woman.

"I can't believe you didn't tell me." It had to be the third time I'd made the proclamation.

Apparently, Jo had "accidently" let it slip during the photo shoot that she'd had a vision of Cliff and Tricia together.

We sat in my Jeep in the Dana Point Marina parking lot and watched Cliff's unattended yacht docked in the west basin. We'd pulled in at six o'clock. Sunset was in thirty minutes. We didn't have a lot of time.

Most people were heading to the restaurants for dinner. If it was a little darker, I'd feel more comfortable climbing aboard. Or, as Darby called it, breaking and entering.

Darby raised her binoculars and focused on the yacht. "I thought Jo was lying. Why would Cliff and Tricia be having an affair?"

"For Cliff it would be a way to get back at Mona. Did you ever consider Tricia might be the reason for Mona and Cliff's break up?" Rumor around town had been Mona had caught him with another woman.

She lowered the binoculars. "Best friends don't steal each other's husbands."

"Those are your midwestern morals talking. Line up ten couples you know from Orange County, and I bet you a minimum of six couples have cheated on each other at some point."

She shook her head. "I refuse to believe it."

A couple who looked like they hadn't seen the light of day since the inauguration of the first President George Bush wobbled past us in matching nautical outfits. The old man squinted through his glasses into the Jeep, checking us out. I smiled and waved, hoping he'd realize there was nothing to see and keep plodding past us.

"Look at Caro," I said. "Her ex had cheated before they'd celebrated their second wedding anniversary. Heck, for all she knows he had never been faithful."

Caro and her ex-husband, Geoff, had met in college while pursuing their psych degrees. (Just the way he spelled his name screamed pretentious butthead. You'd think someone as smart as Caro would have seen that red flag, but she hadn't.)

They'd started a counseling practice together, and before you could say, "It's all your mother's fault," Geoff had taken up with a client. After a public scandal big enough to rival my own public humiliation, Caro and Butthead had lost their licenses.

It doesn't get much worse than that.

"That doesn't explain Tricia," Darby argued.

"She wants to be Mona so badly, she'd take her leftovers. Sad, but true."

My cell chirped from inside my purse, cutting off whatever argument Darby was about to voice. I grabbed my phone and saw it was a text from Grey. He wanted to meet for dinner. I quickly tapped in my reply and hit send.

"Everything okay?" she asked.

"Grey wants to make me dinner."

"Are you going to tell him what we're doing?"

I assumed she meant breaking onto Cliff's boat, not debating couple faithfulness in the OC. "Yes."

I turned on the satellite radio and flipped stations before settling on classic rock. Queen's *I Want To Break Free* reverberated around us.

Darby drummed her fingers on her leg. "I can't sit here any longer. Are we going aboard or not? If we wait too long, it will be dark, and we won't be able to see a thing. Either that or Cliff will come home." She grabbed the door handle.

I really liked the song and thought it was quite fitting for the situation, but for sanity's sake I turned off the radio. "Okay. Let's do it."

We hopped out of the Jeep and quickly made our way toward the dock. I'm sure we looked ridiculous dressed in all black like cat burglars . . . or yoga escapees. We were sporting our yoga garb.

A chill hung in the evening air. We casually strolled past the trendy shops and headed for the area Camilla had described when I'd called her earlier for Cliff's slip number.

As we neared the dock, I could see we'd have to pass through a chain-link security gate. "Camilla failed to mention we needed a key to get to Cliff's boat," I said softly, looking around for a different way to reach our destination.

The older couple who'd shuffled past the Jeep earlier suddenly emerged from the other side of the gate, leaving the dock area. I quickly grabbed the gate before it shut, denying us access.

"I saw you resting in your car," the old man wheezed. "What's a matter? Did you girls work too hard at your calisthenics?" He chuckled, then erupted into a coughing fit strong enough to shoot his dentures across the marina.

"That's what you get." His wife pounded his frail back with an aged hand. "Leave those poor girls alone." She bobbed with every swat, shaking the lopsided bun of white hair pinned precariously on the crown of her head.

"Do you need help?" Darby asked.

A well-practiced apologetic smile pulled at the old woman's orange lipstick-stained mouth. "He'll be fine. He gets excited when he sees a pretty girl."

Darby insisted we watch them as they slowly made their way to a park bench. Once they were seated, I let the gate slam behind us.

"We're in," I whispered. "Let's go."

It was a clear evening, and a large number of boats were still out on the ocean. Water slapped against the wood pier. I inhaled the ocean air, savoring the delicate salt sting as my lungs filled.

We quickly found dock B. *The Ruthless* was easy to spot. At fifty feet, she was one of the larger yachts anchored.

"Cliff, are you home?" I called out just to make sure he wasn't below deck sleeping. Or drinking, which was more likely in his case.

There was no answer. I grabbed the side of the boat and climbed onto the back. The swaying motion tossed me to the side. It took me a second to steady myself. Once I had my sea legs under me, I motioned for Darby to join me.

We made our way past the deck patio and down into the salon. It wasn't a huge area, but big enough for a couple of leather barrel chairs, a sofa and a pop-up TV.

Oh, and a wet bar of multiple Scotches that could rival any liquor store.

The rhythmic rocking helped calm my racing heart. "It's much smaller than the ocean-side mansion, but Mona's money bought him a nice place to crash."

"Let's get this over with. What exactly are we looking for?" Darby's voice shook, her nerves getting the best of her.

"I don't know. Anything that proves he's been gambling or that he killed Mona."

I started in the galley (I knew that was the name for the kitchen, but that was the extent of my proper boat vernacular), and Darby searched the couple of cabinets in the salon (okay, I knew that too).

"Explain to me again, why the police aren't doing this?" she asked.

"Maybe they have."

"Not to be a total wet blanket, but if they didn't find anything, what makes you think we will?"

I glanced sideways at Darby. "Do you have this sudden passion to go to jail?"

"Of course not."

"Okay, stop talking and get looking."

I leafed through a stack of papers on the kitchen table and didn't see anything except past due bills. I opened drawers and only found flatware and dishes. No real food. Nothing.

We were losing light fast. "We'll have to turn on a lamp."

We each tuned on a table lamp in the area we were searching. I quickly moved to one of the sleeping quarters. No photo albums or handwritten notes. Nothing but clothes, sheets and towels. Not even a computer.

"Anything?" I asked, utterly disappointed.

"Not yet."

Either the police had already been here or Cliff didn't have anything to hide (I found the latter hard to believe). I opened a small closet behind the door, and something large and heavy covered with a white sheet tumbled onto my foot. "Ow!"

Darby rushed up and peered around me. I peeled back the sheet.

"Why would Cliff store his paintings in a closet?" she asked.

I pointed to the "walls" which were basically windows. "He doesn't really have a place to hang that type of stuff."

"True." She shrugged and went back to her search.

Was that why Mona had left him her art, because she knew he didn't have a way to appreciate it? Talk about cold hearted.

I continued to stare at the paintings. They looked so familiar. A couple of watercolors and an oil, all three different sizes and different artists. All were dramatic landscapes with excellent contrasting of light and dark. I looked at the signature on the smaller framed oil painting. Thomas Cole.

"I think these are the same paintings Mona had in her bedroom."

"He has a copy?" she asked from the other end of the yacht.

"This is really confusing. Why would Mona leave him her art, if he already owned the same piece? Can you own the same piece? I wish Grey was here."

"Mel, I think I found something in a nightstand," Darby's excited voice pierced my confusion.

She raced to my side and held out a brown Moleskin notebook. We held it under the light and flipped through the pages. It looked like recordings of betting entries, winnings, losses, names and dates.

What jumped out at me was that losses outnumbered the wins. By a huge margin.

I whistled softly. "He owes a lot of money."

"But if he owed money, wouldn't killing Mona be a bad idea?"

"When I called him about Fluffy, he made the comment that Mona hadn't paid him in a while. What if Mona was paying off his gambling debts to save face, then decided she'd had enough and stopped enabling the louse?" I said.

"Or she couldn't give him money because she was broke."

"Exactly. He'd be mad and desperate. Especially if he was stupid enough to take mob money to pay his gambling debts."

"He could be in serious trouble."

"I agree. If he thought he'd get Fluffy, and her money, after Mona's death, that's a strong motive for murder."

"Do you think Malone knows about this?" Darby asked.

"If he doesn't he's going to."

"What about the paintings?"

I pulled out my cell phone and snapped a couple of pictures. "We can't take those with us."

The Yacht tipped to the side, throwing us against the closet.

"You're sure you saw someone over here?" a male voice drifted down toward us.

"Someone's here," Darby said.

"Hide," I croaked.

Rooted in place, we looked around. There was nowhere to hide one person, let alone two. We were about to get caught red-handed.

"I'm *so* going to jail," Darby cried.

Galvanized into action, I shoved the paintings back into the closet.

"I'm positive," a soft female voice assured the man.

I immediately recognized that breathy voice. Tova. What the heck was she doing here?

"Mr. Michaels, is that you?" the man called out.

She'd brought company. The boat continued to sway as the two boarded. I held my index finger over my lips. Darby's eyes looked like they were about to pop out of her head.

I pointed toward the sleeping area, motioning for her to stay there. She shook her head frantically.

"Who's down there?" he demanded.

"I swear I saw two people," Tova's voice drifted into our hiding place.

I'd kill her. We were going to get caught because of dingbat Tova.

"Stay," I whispered.

I brushed past Darby and skittered toward the stairs. "Hello," I called out. "Are you looking for Cliff, too?" I stumbled into a doughy-faced kid who looked like he was fresh out of security training school. The name tag sewn to his uniform read, "Bruce."

"Who are you?" he asked, his voice breaking on "you." He cleared his throat.

"Where's Cliff?" Tova asked at the same time, clutching a wicker patio chair as the boat continued to rock.

Obviously, she wasn't surprised to see me. "I don't know. I've been waiting for him. I needed to talk to him about Fluffy."

"Dressed in all black?" Bruce eyed me with a large amount of skepticism.

"I had a yoga class."

"Mel has bad fashion sense. Everyone knows that." Tova's lame explanation was the least of her problems. Each time the boat swayed she'd stumble, struggling to find her sea legs.

"You know her?" Bruce asked Tova.

My eyes narrowed in Dingbat's direction. Was it my imagination or was she looking slightly green? "What are you doing here?" I asked.

"I'm thinking about buying a sailboat, and Cliff offered to help me," Tova's voice quivered. She gulped a couple of times.

"Really?" I glanced at the death grip she had on the chair. "You're not exactly dressed for yacht shopping."

My comment allowed Bruce the opportunity to openly gawk at Tova. His eyes devoured her model shape tightly wrapped in a short tweed skirt, draped t-shirt that more than hinted at her cleavage, and a pair of suede knee-hi boots.

I didn't believe for a minute she was in the market for a yacht. "Why are you following me?"

Her eyes widened. "I-I didn't."

Bruce's face flashed from outraged to injured. "You followed her? Are you playin' me?"

She started to shake her head, then stopped abruptly. "I-I came by your place to talk about, well, you know . . ." She swallowed and swayed slightly. "I saw you and—" she covered her mouth.

"Bruce, you'd better get her off Cliff's yacht. She looks like she's about to throw up." I interrupted before she ratted out Darby. And she really did look like she was about to puke.

He forgot all about me as he helped Dingbat Tova to dry land. I waited until they were a few yards down the dock before I called out to Darby.

"Coast is clear. Quick, turn off the lights, and let's get out of here."

She bound up the stairs, and we jumped off the yacht. "Where did she come from? Why is she following you?"

"I'm sure it has something to do with my visit with her earlier today."

Tova and I were going to have words later.

Chapter Twenty-Seven

It was completely dark, with only the full moon as a flashlight. It had taken us mere minutes to rush to the Jeep and race back to Laguna. I wasn't sure what had happened to Tova, but I wouldn't be surprised to find out tomorrow that somehow her getting sick would be my fault.

"I can't believe we made it off *Ruthless* without getting into serious trouble. I don't ever want to experience that again." Fear laced Darby's words. Under the streetlights I could see her flushed cheeks.

"Definitely a close call." Unlike my best friend, I liked the adrenalin rush. I felt like I could run a marathon in record time. "You put Cliff's notebook back where you found it, right?" I asked.

"Yes. Are you going to call Malone tomorrow?"

"Absolutely."

Speaking of calling, my cell rang just as we entered Laguna city limits. I fumbled around in my purse, not wanting to miss Grey's call. I was running late to dinner. I glanced at the number as I answered. It wasn't Grey. I turned on my hands-free.

"Hey, Mama," I kept my voice light.

"Why haven't you called?" her voice cracked with tension.

"I did. I left a message."

"You could have tried again. I raised you better than that."

I kept my eyes on the road and pressed the accelerator harder. "I sent you a text."

"You should have standards, Melinda. Texting promotes bad spelling and bad grammar. I heard about your little friend. Did you know she was Mona's daughter?"

Apparently the tabloids had caught wind of Darby's parentage. I glanced at "my little friend," who was exerting great effort to not hear my speaker phone conversation. "I had no idea. What about you?"

"I knew Mona had a child, but I had no idea whether her unfortunate offspring was a boy or girl."

The passenger-side tire blipped off the shoulder for a brief second. Darby scrambled for something to brace herself.

"What is it with y'all?" I shouted. "How many more secrets are going to come out before this is over?" I could feel Darby's stare.

"Everyone has secrets," Mama's voice sizzled with exasperation.

"What do you need, Mama?"

I could hear the faint sound of drumming fingers. "Did you find your brother? Do I need to call the FBI? The National Guard?" she asked as I pulled into my driveway.

There was a car I didn't recognize parked behind Darby's Fiesta across the street. It couldn't be Tova's. It was way too modest.

"Mama, hold on a second. Darby, do you know whose car that is?" I whispered.

There was just enough light from the street lamp that I could see her shake her head. "No."

I had a bad feeling. "Lord have mercy," I muttered.

"Melinda, what's going on?"

"I said, just a minute, Mama." I took a breath. "*Please.*"

My heart raced as the driver's door opened, and the inside light flicked on. A tall, dark haired man stepped out. Then the passenger door opened, and a leggy brunette joined him. Their doors closed in stereo, filling the quiet neighborhood. He said something to her over the top of the car, and she smiled. My stomach dropped.

"Mama, I've got to go. I'll call you later."

"Melinda, what—" I disconnected as she continued to talk.

"Do you know them?" Darby asked, watching from the side mirror as they crossed the street to the driveway.

My heart was beating in my throat. I swallowed past it. "The good looking idiot in the suit is my brother." I turned off the engine when I realized it was still running.

"I'll be going," Darby said, clambering from the Jeep.

"Yeah, that's probably a good idea."

We got out, and I waited for bad news to meet me in the driveway. Darby immediately made a beeline for her car. She waved as she drove off without a backwards glance. Coward.

My brother, who hasn't hugged me since the day he left home, wrapped his arms around me and squeezed, lifting me off my feet. Not an easy task.

"What's wrong," I managed to force out.

"Nothing." He let go and stepped back. "You look good, Mel. Were you at an exercise class?"

I felt a tad awkward in my yoga getup with these two dressed for a date at the symphony. "Something like that. You've been off the Mama radar. What's going on?"

His lopsided smile was forced, as if he was nervous and unsure of his reception. "Nikki, this is my little sister, Melinda."

Nikki was not southern. My bad feeling metamorphosed into relief. A wave of giddiness washed over me. Mitch was fine. He was more than fine.

And Mama was going to throw a Texas-sized fit.

Nikki held out her slender hand, which I quickly accepted. Her grip was firm but not competitive. Impressive. Even in the dark I could see she oozed exotic beauty.

She tipped her head sideways and offered a genuine smile. "I've heard a lot about you. I hope you don't mind we showed up unannounced. I told Mitch we should have called first. It looked like you were in the middle of something."

An intimate look passed between them that spoke volumes. She was chastising Mitch.

"Excuse us for one moment." I grabbed my brother by the arm and dragged him toward the front door. I looked back one last time at the woman who probably wasn't a Vegas showgirl. Knowing my brother, she'd graduated from Brown, top of her class. But that wouldn't matter to our Mama.

I held back the smile that was itching to escape. "Mitchell, tell me."

He smiled sheepishly. "I wanted you to be the first to meet my wife, Nikki Langston."

"Oh my gawd. Mama's gonna have your hide," my southern accent had landed. I let out a Texas whoop my Daddy'd be proud of.

I was *so* out of Mama's crosshairs for a good six months.

Chapter Twenty-Eight

It's funny how some things just work themselves out. Being the wonderfully supportive little sister I am, I relinquished my house to the newest Langstons and ordered Mitch to call the folks. It was time to break the horrific news—there would be no Dallas wedding.

Not only that, Nikki's full name was Nicole Rosa Isabel Espinoza Langston. I couldn't wipe the gratified smile off my face. If I hadn't been in the middle of my own ridiculous drama, I would have hopped on the first plane to Dallas to witness Mama's meltdown. Trust me, there will be fireworks of epic proportions. And for once, I wasn't the target.

Don't misunderstand, it's not Nikki's nationality that will throw Mama into a conniption fit, it's the competing heritage traditions. In Dallas, charity events, parties and weddings are a reflection of your reputation.

Mitch had every reason to be wary of Mama.

Now that my brother's alien behavior had an explanation, it was time to concentrate on the rest of my life, which was spiraling down the crazy drain.

My best friend was still the number one suspect in the murder of a local pseudo-celebrity. I was still guardian of a high maintenance dog. And I was still being sued.

I did what any semi-sane person would do. I headed for The Top of The World. I followed the twisting curves higher and higher, the night breeze dancing through the palm trees.

Unlike Tova's desert landscaping, Grey's had curb appeal. A potpourri of impatiens, cosmos and petunias with a handful of mini palm trees as accents. I pulled into the driveway and shut off the Jeep. I faced my four-legged passengers. Missy, who rode shotgun, knew exactly where we were and was eager to show Grey some love.

"Missy, you already know the rules." I turned to Her Highness. "Fluffy, here's what you need to know. Stay off the couch. Stay off our bed. Grey bought you a bed. Use it."

Fluffy sat at attention, her long nose pointed toward Missy, but her eyes questioning me.

"She's not allowed on the couch or bed either." Sheesh. I hadn't realized dogs could experience sibling rivalry.

Missy pranced in the seat, anxious to unload. I reached over to release the harness just as she sneezed. Bulldog drool shot out all over the inside of the Jeep and onto me.

"Yuck." I pulled out a box of tissues from the middle console and wiped her sticky chin. Behind me, Fluffy rubbed her nose with her paw. She'd also been a causality of Missy snot.

I gently held her narrow face and cleaned her off. She watched me, not sure what I was about. "There you go, girlfriend."

I scratched the top of her head and kissed her lightly. Fluffy licked my cheek, then turned away as if embarrassed.

I winked at Missy. "Well, well, well. Looks like Her Highness is warming up to us." I rubbed Missy's head and gave her a few kisses, too, not wanting her to feel left out of the love fest.

"Alrighty then." I wadded the tissues into a ball and shoved them back into the console. "Let's hit it, ladies."

I slung my Louis Vuitton travel bag over my shoulder and raced the dogs up the stone walkway. We'd made it halfway to the house, when the front door swung open.

"I see you brought friends." Grey's deep voice made me feel a little dizzy.

He looked like home in his jeans, black t-shirt and mussed hair, and he smelled like dinner. More specifically, garlic mashed potatoes. My stomach growled.

"Never leave a soldier behind." I planted a quick kiss on his mouth.

The dogs raced through the doorway. Missy immediately headed for her bed. Fluffy had no idea where she was going, but she wasn't about to be left out. She immediately started her own investigation, starting with the kitchen.

Grey locked the door for the night, then grabbed my bag and tossed it on the bench in the hallway. "Must be serious. Louis's heavy."

"Mitch brought a wife."

He grinned and raised his brow. "He was living a secret life."

I nodded. "Nikki Rosa Isabel Espinoza Langston. I can already hear Mama. 'What kind of name is that? Is she a prostitute? You cannot have an *ethnic* wedding.'"

He draped his arm over my shoulders and tucked me close to his side. He was the only man I'd ever dated who could make me feel petite.

"Poor Mitch."

"He's a big boy. He knew what he was doing. I feel bad for Nikki, she's very nice. But it's better for her to know the real Barbara Langston."

"She does take some getting used to."

"Amen. I'm sorry we're so late. Have you already eaten?"

"I waited."

We headed for the kitchen where he'd prepared an amazing dinner of grilled salmon, steamed broccoli and those garlic smashed potatoes I already mentioned. In the center of the round glass table sat a bottle of my favorite Pinot Noir.

I kissed him on the cheek. "I am the luckiest woman alive. It smells delicious." I washed my hands at the kitchen sink. "Today was kinda wild. You wouldn't believe it."

He pulled out my chair. "Try me."

We sat, and Grey poured the wine. His shirt sleeves were casually rolled to his elbows, exposing his forearm muscles. He placed my glass next to my plate, then poured some for himself.

I rested my chin in the palm of my hands and stared at him. I took a deep breath and savored the moment. "I've missed you."

He looked over the rim of his wine glass; his eyes promised to make it up to me.

I shivered. "Stop it." I tore my gaze away from his face and concentrated on my dinner. "This is so delicious. I just realized I haven't eaten since breakfast."

"Something kept you away from food?" He chuckled.

I savored a fork full of potatoes, then launched into my day. "First, Owen summoned a small group to his office this afternoon to inform us Mona was broke. So broke, she'd filed bankruptcy last month."

"I'm sorry I missed that meeting."

"Liar," I said around a mouthful of salmon. I swallowed and then continued, "He gave me a copy of Mona's will. She named me Fluffy's guardian."

"You get Fluffy?"

"Her well laid out plan of revenge. As her new owner, it's my job to find her a bodyguard. Interested?"

His lips twitched. "No. Why does she need a bodyguard now?"

I pointed a floweret of broccoli at him. "I have no idea."

I filled him in on the meeting and explained about the insurance money for both Darby and Fluffy. By time I was finished, so was dinner.

"How's Darby holding up?" He leaned back in his chair and sipped his wine.

"She wouldn't tell you, but not good." I placed my utensils on my empty plate and pushed it aside. "I want to tell you something—a number of somethings. But you have to promise not to get upset until after I tell you everything."

Grey pushed his plate aside too and sighed knowingly. He looked at me in that way that said he was done arguing. "I'm not sure I want to make that promise."

"I didn't say you couldn't get upset." We both knew that was a given. "Just wait until I'm finished. Then you can yell at me." I shot him a self-deprecating grin.

I downplayed Darby's and my excellent adventure of breaking and entering (I used very passive verbs), but I was a good girl and didn't leave out a single detail.

The muscle in his check twitched, and his green eyes sparkled with a great deal of irritation. But being the gentleman he was, he didn't say a word. Yet.

When I admitted to poking my nose into Malone's investigation, I thought he was going to explode like Old Faithful. "I promise I'm going to call Malone first thing in the morning and let him know about Cliff's notebook."

"I specifically said to stay away from Cliff." His curt tone was not for show.

I had the stray thought that the make up sex tonight would be great. But I didn't think he wanted to hear that right now.

"He wasn't there. I swear."

Under the table my legs pumped up and down with a life of their own. "Oh, and I have something I want you to look at." I hopped up and grabbed my cell.

Spilling my guts to Grey had been more emotional than I'd expected. To be honest, I hadn't really given it much thought. Oh, I'd known he'd be upset, but I figured he'd get over it. By the look on his face when I'd left the table, he didn't look like he wanted to get over it anytime soon.

I came back with reinforcements—the dogs.

"You're not going to stop this, are you?" He gathered the plates and carried them to the sink, clearly upset and exasperated.

The dogs sniffed the floor beneath the table looking for leftovers. Fluffy was so bold to actually sniff the table. Bad dog.

"I can't."

"Is this because of Caro?" Grey began loading the dishwasher with his back to me.

It was a simple question, and I understood why he was asking.

"Not at all. This is because Darby's innocent." I set my phone on the counter and helped him load the dishes. We worked in silence.

Once we finished, I said softly, "I need your help."

"I know." He leaned his back against the counter and tucked his fingers in his pockets. He wasn't happy. "I'm more than a little upset, Mel." I opened my mouth to answer, but he raised his hand for me to keep quiet. "But I know you're going to do what you want. The only way I can reassure myself you're not going to run head first into trouble is to do what I can to help."

Jubilation exploded like a fireworks finale. I jumped him right there in the kitchen and peppered his face with kisses.

He finally broke down and laughed. "All right, get off me."

I wiggled my eyebrows. "I bet you never thought you'd say that to me?"

I dropped to the floor and grabbed my cell. I pulled up the photos of Cliff's paintings. "What do you make of this?"

I handed my phone to Grey just as his doorbell rang.

"Got another hot date tonight?" I asked.

He handed my phone back. "I can only handle one crazy woman at a time," he said wryly.

Ironic really, because who was on the other side of the door? Dingbat Tova.

"I'd like to see Melinda." Her voice was unrecognizably confident.

I strolled to the door, guard up. "Hey. How'd you know where to find me?"

She'd changed out of her seduce-newly-trained-security guard outfit and into a powder blue sweat suit and pumps. "I saw your car. I'll take the fifteen hundred dollars. A check is fine."

Grey looked at me questioningly.

"I'll fill you in later," I said. To Tova I clarified one more time, "I'm not apologizing."

She rolled her shoulders back. "I know."

I narrowed my eyes. "I'm not admitting to the fleas."

She sighed, her face pinched into acceptance. "Just mail the check. I've already called my attorney to drop the lawsuit."

I channeled my gracious winner face. But let's be honest, inside I was a fist pumping freak. "Will do," I said, straight-faced.

Tova turned around and runway-walked back to her Hummer.

I closed the door and let out my second Texas holler of the day.

"What was that about?" Grey asked amused.

"I found a way to get her to drop the lawsuit." I preformed my celebratory dance with a few "whoop whoops" thrown in. I was quite proud of myself.

"You have been busy. What did you have to do?"

My party fizzled. "Pay her the original fifteen hundred dollars. But she's cost me that much in just annoyance."

"I'm proud of you, Babe. You're dealing with an irrational person. That wasn't going to change. You'd have paid more in legal fees. You did what you had to."

I puffed out my chest and shot him a cocky grin. "Thanks, *Babe*."

He held out his hand. "Let me see the phone."

I pulled it out of my pocket and found the pictures again. This time my cell rang, interrupting us. "What in the world . . ." I looked up at Grey. "It's Tricia. Why would she call me?"

"Answer it, and let's find out," he said.

Chapter Twenty-Nine

"Melinda?" Tricia wailed over the phone. "I need your help."

I headed to the great room and plopped on one of the two couches. Grey and the dogs followed.

She's crying, I mouthed to Grey. He looked mildly curious. I just shrugged.

"This is a little awkward, Tricia. I don't normally discuss business after hours." I picked up a decorative pillow and tossed it aside, making room for Grey. I flashed him an inviting smile.

He sat next to me, and Missy immediately curled up at his feet. Fluffy stayed back and watched.

"This isn't about the clothing line," she simpered. "I don't know what to do. I'm scared."

I rolled my eyes in disbelief. "Scared of what?"

"Not what. Who," her tone sharp. "Jo came at me like a mafia wife in the Whole Food's parking lot tonight."

I choked back laughter. "What are you talking about?" I put her on speaker phone so Grey could hear.

"She was waiting for me at my car. She yelled obscenities at me. Can you believe it? Then she said I'd be sorry if I didn't help her."

A big piece of the puzzle was missing. "Does this have to do with what you two were arguing about in the bathroom?"

Grey quietly got up and left the room. Fluffy tagged along. Missy readjusted until she was lying on my foot and resumed snoring.

"Yes." She sniffed. "She lost something in Mona's car and wanted to know if I could retrieve it for her."

Why would Tricia do anything out of the goodness of her heart for Jo? Unless she owed Jo a favor. "What did she lose?"

Grey came back to the room with a pad of paper. He'd scribbled one word. Blackmail.

I looked at him and nodded, impressed. Damn, he was smart.

"I-I can't tell you," she hedged.

"Is Jo blackmailing you?" I tried to sound caring, but I think it came across as almost an accusation. I needed to work on my delivery.

There was a moment of silence. "Yes."

Ding, ding, ding. We have ourselves a winner. Grey's eyes widened in triumph. We shared an air fist bump.

"Is this about your 'date' the night Mona was murdered?" I asked.

"What?"

Clearly Tricia wasn't the brainy type. "Are you dating a married man? Is that what Jo's blackmailing you with?"

A sigh of annoyance rushed across the phone. "Apparently, you've never been blackmailed before. Part of the instructions are don't go to the police and don't talk to anyone."

"Tricia, you're smarter than this. You can't possibly take Jo seriously?"

"What if she killed Mona?"

"I thought you believed Cliff or his brother, Ted, killed her?"

"I've changed my mind. I think it was Jo. I didn't tell you this, but Mona fired her."

I sat up abruptly, accidently kicking Missy. She didn't move. "When?

"The day of the Fur Ball," she announced dramatically.

She enjoyed piecing out her information bit by bit.

"Tricia, I have to go. You're going to be fine. First thing tomorrow, visit Malone. Tell him everything you just told me. He'll help you."

I disconnected before she could protest.

"If she actually goes to see Malone tomorrow, that should help Darby, right?" I asked Grey.

"Possibly," he replied cautiously. "Don't be surprised if she doesn't go. If Jo really is holding something over her, the shame of being exposed can outweigh the fear toward the blackmailer."

"Well, that's dumb. Tricia shouldn't have been carrying on with some married man."

Grey was reflective. "She never said that's what Jo was holding over her head. You assumed that's what it was."

Really? I thought about it for a second, and he was right. I'd actually suggested it. "If not that, then what?"

Grey dropped down next to me and held out his palm. "Let me see those pictures before your phone rings again."

I quickly pulled up the photos and showed Grey. "Aren't those the same ones that were at Mona's?"

He didn't say anything as he flipped back and forth between the pictures. I watched him send copies to his personal email. "Where'd you find these?" he asked.

"On Cliff's yacht in his closet." I rubbed Missy's back with my foot. "Where's Fluffy?"

"She went upstairs," he answered absently.

Great. Probably looking for an escape route.

"How can they both have the same painting?" I asked, looking over his shoulder.

He handed the phone back to me. "Either they're both copies or one's the original, and the other is a copy."

"How do we find which one it is?

"We don't. I will. You talk to Jo and find out if Tricia was telling the truth."

"You think Tricia's lying?"

"I think Tricia was groomed by Mona. Tricia has an agenda, and I want to find out what it is."

That made sense. First she said she was looking for a contract, then she claimed Jo was blackmailing her. Supposedly for dating a married man. Not to sound callous, but unless that married man is either a celebrity or politician, no one cared.

Tomorrow would be an interesting day.

Chapter Thirty

I'd overslept. While I showered, Grey walked the dogs. Even though he'd poked fun at the weight of my bag, I really hadn't brought a lot of clothing choices. The weight came from my boots.

I pulled on my jeans and a tunic sweater. After running a wide-tooth comb through my wet hair, I secured the thick mess in a bun. I grabbed my boots and scurried downstairs inhaling the smell of coffee and burned eggs.

I found Grey and the dogs in the kitchen. Grey reading the paper, Missy eating her food, and Fluffy . . . well, I wasn't sure what she was doing. It looked like she was gazing longingly out the patio door.

"She's tracking the neighbor's cat," Grey said from behind the paper.

"Good to know. Got any hot water?" I pulled a travel mug from the cupboard.

"I left a mug for you in the microwave. Lemons in the fridge."

I found my hot water where he'd left it. Some day I'd learn to like coffee like the other grown-ups. "Did any eggs survive?" The non-stick pan in the sink hadn't lived up to its reputation. Grey had killed it.

"Nope. I got distracted," he offered as an explanation for the black mess in the sink. "You wanna grab something in town?"

I heard the paper rustle behind me. I checked my watch. It was after nine, and I wanted to talk to Jo as soon as possible. "I'm good. I'll probably just grab a drink at the Koffee Klatch. Dinner?"

"Are you offering to cook?" He dropped the paper on the glass table.

He hadn't overslept. He looked refreshed, clean shaven and dressed for the gallery.

"Nope. I'm offering to eat with you."

He chuckled. "It's a date."

I gave him a big smooch and agreed to call him later. "Let's go, dogs."

The three of us loaded into the Jeep and sped off to my place to drop off my furry passengers. Then I was off to Caro's. It was time to get my brooch back.

Unlike my cousin, I didn't have to break into her home. I'd taken the liberty of having a copy of her key made. (Now, don't act so shocked. If we were on speaking terms, you know I'd be the first person she'd entrust with a spare.)

Once I was certain she wasn't home, I walked the half block to her place. (I wasn't so bold that I'd park in her driveway; the goal was to get in and out without being caught.) I unlocked the door and walked inside.

Dogbert, a rescue mixed-breed, barked his welcome. His bark was definitely terrier. It had that sharp tone that said he was boss. I got down on one knee and pulled out the bacon flavored treats I'd brought just for Dog.

"Here you go, boy." I fed him one. Once he'd finished it, he immediately rolled over for a belly rub. I willingly obliged.

As I gave Dog his rub down, I casually looked around. Her open floor plan was both a blessing and a curse when looking for my brooch.

Thelma and Louise, her cats, were stretched out along the top of the overstuffed couch sunbathing. Where would Caro have hid it this time? It was possible she had it with her. Probably not. She'd be worried about the gems coming loose.

I stood and walked into the kitchen.

Her organized cupboards were stocked with health food. Where's the sugar, Sugar? I opened the fridge and was equally disappointed.

"Well, I'm glad you haven't invited me over for dinner. Yikes. I'm not sure I'd survive on tuna and organic veggies."

Thelma and Louise meandered through the kitchen, swishing between my feet checking out what I was doing.

"Ladies, I brought a little something for you too."

I pulled out at pouch of Kitty Kat Kibbles and poured out two small piles on the counter, one for each of them.

Maybe she hid the pin in her bedroom.

As I was passing through the living room, I noticed her overstuffed bookcase was even more overstuffed than the last time I'd visited. I didn't normally notice that type of stuff, but Caro always had interesting books. And a wide variety. Fiction, non-fiction, reference, and her favorite biographies. She loved to read.

There were two new books shoved on top of the other books that had caught my attention. They looked like text books. Being the nosy cousin, I helped myself to see what she'd bought this time. *Relational Diagnosis and Dysfunctional Family Patterns* and *Diagnostic and Statistical Manual of Mental Disorders.*

Obviously she was researching our family tree.

I pulled the fancy burgundy leather book off the shelf. It looked like it was from her therapy days. Not when she was in therapy, but when she was paid to give out advice. It smelled kinda musty. Eew.

I ran my hand over the leather. It was soft and in decent shape. I opened the cover thinking I might find something to help me deal with Mama and almost dropped it.

"Oh, no, you didn't."

Caro had defaced a book.

My cousin, the lover of all things bookish had ripped out a handful of pages and taped something wrapped in a monogrammed hankie (CAL) to the inside cover. That something was the exact size as Grandma Tillie's brooch. My snoopiness paid off big time.

My heart surged with excitement.

Very carefully, I removed my prized possession and unwrapped it. Not a loose gem on it. Perfectly garish. And all mine. I gave it an appreciative smooch.

It was back where it belonged.

"You are one sneaky gal, Carolina Alexis Lamont."

Chapter Thirty-One

This time I wasn't taking any chances. I headed home to hide my loot in a secure place. Fluffy's safe. I tucked away the pin next to Fluffy's own prized treasures. I have to admit I felt a little cocky for once again being on top. It was going to be a great day.

Mitch and Nikki had left a note letting me know they were out for a morning stroll on the beach. I was about to call the dogs, but realized they were crashed out in their beds. I scribbled a note to the newlyweds that I'd check on the furry kids after noon and scrammed.

With an enormous smile on my face, I sped down PCH toward the shop. I spied Cliff's Land Rover at Nick's restaurant. Without a second thought, I cranked the steering wheel to the left and parked.

As soon as I climbed out of the Jeep, the powerful aroma of fried chicken and coffee assaulted my sensibilities. My stomach growled, demanding to be fed. Nick's was one of the few restaurants in town where you'd find an entree of fried chicken and gravy with waffles on the menu.

It was a nice place with trendy deco and good food. At times a long wait to get into for dinner. Especially during tourist season.

I walked inside and spotted Cliff sitting at the bar, no breakfast. Unless you considered a Bloody Mary the breakfast of champions. I claimed the barstool next to him.

"What the hell do you want?" he growled.

Someone woke up on the wrong side of the bed this morning. I took in his mussed hair and scruffy face. He was wearing the same bowling shirt he'd worn yesterday. Correction. Someone still needed to go to bed.

"Long night?" I asked.

"Whada you care?" He drank deeply, almost stabbing himself in the eye with the celery stick sticking out of his glass.

"I hear you're in trouble."

"What do you know about it?" he snapped.

I waved the bartender over and asked for an iced tea. His gaze shifted between Cliff and me but wisely kept his opinion to himself.

"I guess you're the last to know. It's well known around town you've got a gambling problem."

An awkward moment passed. The bartender brought my tea, then vanished.

Cliff shrugged. "So I gamble. What's the big deal?"

"I'd say borrowing money from Batty is a big deal," I whispered.

His glass slid from his hand, landing upright on the bar. He whipped around and glared at me. "Are you trying to get us killed?"

Lord, he could get angry fast. Imagine how angry he could be at someone he hated. I moved him to the top of my suspect list. "If you're that afraid of him, why on God's green earth would you take money from him?"

"I didn't."

It took me a second, but I got it. "Ted."

"This is all Mona's fault. If she hadn't gone back on her word, I wouldn't be in the mess."

"What part did she go back on?" Fluffy or paying him off in cash?

He motioned for the bartender to bring him another Bloody Mary. "Up until a month ago, she was giving me money."

"That doesn't sound like Mona."

"I had a little leverage." He leered at me as if I should be impressed with the revelation. "She was leading a fictional lifestyle. You know what I mean?"

Her and sixty percent of the US population. Way too many people living beyond what they could afford. "So you were blackmailing her?"

"Not at all. We had an agreement. Then she stopped paying me."

"Why? Because you were sleeping with her best friend?"

He blinked, then laughed. Loudly. You know that annoying drunk-guy laugh? Only I don't think he was drunk. Yet.

"Whoever told you I was boffing Tricia is crazy. I had the real deal, and I couldn't stand her. Why would I want a cheap imitation?"

Wow. That was harsh. Accurate, but harsh nonetheless.

"So you threatened Mona?" I asked.

A rather charming smile appeared, and, for a moment, I caught a glimpse of what Mona may have seen in him. Then he opened his mouth. "I explained the situation. And out of the goodness of her heart she started paying me again."

He was so lying. He was trying too hard to convince me.

"How'd she find the money?"

"How should I know? I didn't care as long as I was getting what she owed me. She still owes me that dog."

"You're not getting Fluffy."

"I'll sue you," he tossed out his empty threat.

We both knew he didn't have the resources to take me on. "What's stopping you?" I asked.

He glared at me and chugged the rest of his drink. He wiped his mouth with the back of his hand.

"What about her art?" I asked.

"What about it?" he asked warily.

"Why'd she leave it to you? You live on a yacht."

He sneered, "She had a twisted sense of humor." He slid off the stool and threw a handful of bills on the bar.

"Is that why you killed her?" I asked before he could get away.

He didn't bother to even look at me. "She was my cash cow. Why would I kill her?"

That was a very good question. "Maybe you weren't planning on it. It just happened."

He looked at me in complete seriousness. "Nothing just happened with Mona."

And with that he waltzed out of Nick's as if he didn't have a care in the world. If the mob was after me, I'd be changing zip codes faster than you could say lily-livered pond sucker.

I'd just stepped outside when I heard someone call my name. It was Darby strolling down the PCH sidewalk with Fluffy.

I watched the two come toward me. Apparently Darby woke up this morning thinking she was impersonating Annie Hall in her wide legged trousers, white long-sleeved t-shirt and brown scarf tied around her neck like a tie.

For all their differences, Fluffy and Darby fit together. Her Highness was in go mode, prancing along side Darby. I had to give Fluffy credit for not tugging on the lead. Impressive. It also gave me an idea.

"Why in the world do you have her?" I asked as soon as Darby was within ear shot.

"I stopped by your place when Bow Wow never opened. I was worried." Her face was flush from the brisk walk. For a moment she looked like the Darby I met two years ago. Fresh from the midwest without a care.

"And then what? Her Highness raced out the front door, hopped into your little Fiesta, and demanded that you take her for a walk?" I laughed, thinking about Fluffy riding around Laguna in a Ford. So different than her Jag.

"Not exactly," she hedged. "She doesn't seem to like your brother."

I greeted Snob Dog with a pat. She shook off my show of affection.

"Did he guilt you into taking her?" I asked, offended on my friend's behalf.

"I offered. I'm getting used to her. Was that Cliff driving off?"

"Sure was. He freely admitted he had a gambling problem and was indebted to a certain group of unsavory characters." We fell into step. The Koffee Klatch was behind us, but there was a Starbucks up the street. I could still get my chai.

"Did he explain about the paintings?" she asked.

"No. But Grey's working on that angle for us."

"Grey?" she asked, surprised.

I filled her in on last night. She was also impressed I'd gotten Tova to drop the lawsuit, even if I had to pay her off in the process.

We were standing in line waiting on our Starbucks order when I asked, "How about the three of us visit a certain pet psychic? Mona's last call was to Jo. I want to know what they talked about."

"What if she won't tell you?" Darby asked.

"Then I'll ask her why she's blackmailing Tricia."

Chapter Thirty-Two

It was partly cloudy with a chance of clearing Darby's name. I know, lame. The whole sleuthing gig was going to my head. But I could feel it in my bones. Today we'd dig up some clue to change the direction of Malone's investigation. I still needed to call him.

To be honest, there was never a time I'd thought I'd step foot in Jo's business. In fact, I hadn't known she even worked out of an office building. I just assumed she'd worked out of her home. Imagine my shock to learn she had an office suite right off Forrest. It was so professional of her. So unexpected.

Our little trio squeezed through the door, Fluffy leading the way. This wasn't her first visit. She wasn't tense or showing the need to sniff around and investigate. Unlike me.

Jo stomped down the hallway with a supersized mug in her hand. "What do you want?" she barked.

I felt Darby flinch.

I couldn't stop looking at Jo's hair. Somehow it managed to be a rats nest and stringy simultaneously. It looked horrible. Actually, she looked bad from head to toe. There were dark circles under her eyes, and her shoulders sagged. Her whole demeanor was broken. Blackmailing people must be tiring work. Maybe Malone had already paid her a visit.

I pulled myself together. "We want a reading. Or whatever you call it."

"Bull." Her foghorn voice belted out the one syllable word. She pointed at Fluffy. "You brought the dog. This is a test."

Apparently we were diving right in. "You can look at it that way if you want. But if you can convince me you're legit, what better advertisement is there?"

"I don't do séances." She tilted her chin, daring me to challenge her.

"Neither do I." I shot her my beauty pageant smile.

She rolled her eyes, disgusted.

Hey, that smile had won me a crown or two back in the day.

Jo brushed some crumbs off the front of her black t-shirt. "Fine.

But you have to do what I tell you."

I looked at Darby, and she nodded. "Agreed," I said. Okay, I crossed my fingers behind my back.

We headed down the hallway to her miniature Dr. Phil office. A very long uninviting couch, a couple of overstuffed chairs, end tables. And boxes and boxes of tissues stashed within reach throughout the room. A staple for when you tell your clients they're going to die.

"Sit," Jo ordered.

Fluffy immediately sat on my foot. "Not you, girl." I patted her head.

"Do we take the couch or chairs?" Darby asked.

"Whatever you're comfortable with," Jo replied with a vague wave of her hand.

Darby looked uneasy and headed straight for the couch. I followed her lead. It wasn't my first choice, but hopefully we weren't staying long. Lord have mercy, it was like sitting on plywood. I'd better not have any splinters in my butt by the time we left.

Fluffy paraded over and inched herself up against Darby. I shot a I-see-how-it-is glare at Snob Dog. I swear she smiled back.

Jo warily settled on a chair. She let out a pent up breath, closed her eyes and rolled her shoulders a couple of times.

"Why were you blackmailing Mona?" I asked.

She sighed and shot me a death glare with one eye open. "You're not very good at this. You agreed."

I shrugged. "I crossed my fingers."

Jo opened both eyes. She looked tired, almost as if I'd finally broken her lying spirit. I almost felt sorry for her. Almost.

"I told you I didn't kill Mona. I wasn't blackmailing her, either. Tricia and Cliff were having an affair." She continued to stick to the same story.

"That just doesn't make sense," Darby insisted, stroking Fluffy's head, which was now resting adoringly on Darby's lap. The sweet girl from Nebraska refused to believe a good friend would commit the ultimate betrayal. Man, I loved her spunk.

"Look, Jo. I know you're hiding something. What is it? Where were you the night Mona died?" I asked.

"I was here. Alone."

"No one's going to believe you. Spill it. What are you hiding?" I said.

She rubbed her hands on her jeans. "Mona fired me," she finally admitted.

"I know." Her head shot up, shock clearly stamped on her face. "Tricia told me. Do you want to fill me in on the bathroom argument yet?"

"Why, it sounds like Tricia's already talked enough for the both of us."

"She's going to file a police report. She claims you accosted her in the parking lot last night and are blackmailing her."

Jo swore. Darby covered Fluffy's ears.

"She is such a blabbermouth," Jo complained.

"So it's true?" Darby asked, wide-eyed.

Jo sat forward, nostrils flaring. "No, it's not true. I'm not the one who was blackmailing Mona," she insisted.

No, that was Cliff. The cad boasted about it at breakfast. "But you admit to blackmailing Tricia?"

She looked at Fluffy. "I told you. She was having an affair with Cliff."

I shook my head. "Not according to Cliff. I believe him."

"You've talked to Cliff?" Jo looked shaken. She drummed her finger on the arms of the chair.

I shifted my weight, not exactly comfortable with the wild look developing in Jo's eyes. "A little over an hour ago. He was full of info."

Jo sprang from the chair. Darby gasped and laid a protective hand on Fluffy.

"I'll be right back," Jo said with a forced smile. "I just remembered I didn't set the phones to forward to voicemail." She raced out of the office like a bat from you know where.

I don't know who she thought she was fooling, but it didn't take a medium or a psychic to know she was ducking out. I could hear the back door creaking as she tried to quietly and slowly make her escape.

"She's running." I shouted.

Fluffy barked and charged for the door.

Chapter Thirty-Three

I grabbed Darby, she grabbed Fluffy, and we rushed out the front door. We hid behind a huge black Caddy SUV parked on the street and waited for our escapee. Sure enough, Jo charged out of the backyard without a backwards glance in our direction, wearing dark sunglasses and a leather vest over her t-shirt.

Game on, sister.

The three of us followed up the busy street, weaving around people when needed, sometimes hiding behind them, not wanting to give away our presence. It may not be prime tourist season, but people flocked to Laguna year round.

Jo bobbed around a young couple walking their Great Dane. She glanced over her shoulder. I tried to hide behind the tree, but it was too late, she'd spotted us. Crapola.

Jo picked up speed and was now almost running. I wish I knew where she was running to.

"She did it. She killed Mona." Darby sounded out of breath. From the realization we knew who killed her mother or from the spontaneous cardio exercise, I couldn't tell. I was concentrating on not letting Jo out my sight as we got closer to PCH.

Once Jo reached the corner she cut left. I couldn't see her. Suddenly, there was an ear-piercing scream mixed with the blare of a bus horn.

"No, no, no." I yelled.

I hauled it around the corner trying to catch up to Jo, leaving Darby and Fluffy behind.

A small crowd had gathered in front of the bus, people pulling out their cell phones.

The bus doors swung open, and a short frantic man scurried into the crowd.

"She ran into the street," his panicked voice rang in the air. "I couldn't stop. You saw it, right? Someone tell me you saw her run out in front of me." He yelled at the crowd gathered around the bus. He was the bus driver, Denny, according to his plastic name badge.

He charged up to a young kid standing on his skateboard and grabbed a handful of his shirt. "You saw it happen. She ran out in front of me."

The kid pushed him away. "Dude, you ran over the pet psychic."

Denny suddenly collapsed in a heap onto the sidewalk.

Ambulance and police sirens screeched toward us. Unfortunately, I think Denny would be the only one benefiting from the ambulance headed our way.

"Why would she dart in front of a bus?" someone in the crowd asked.

"I think someone pushed her," a shaky female voice commented behind me.

"Check out that tattoo. Do you think she got it locally?" someone else said, clearly impressed with Lassie (may she rest in peace).

The kid on his skateboard prodded Denny with his foot. "Is he dead, too?"

My stomach was in knots. I looked over at Darby. "Are you okay?"

She nodded, but I could tell she wasn't. She looked like she was about to puke.

My stomach clenched. How in the world was I going to explain this to Grey? The first police car roared up to the crowd and parked in a way to block traffic. What a mess.

Seeing the cop car added a whole new level of anxiety. I chewed my lip. "Lord, I sure hope Malone doesn't show up. Even I can't talk my way out of this one."

Chapter Thirty-Four

Darby had retreated back to her place. She'd taken Fluffy with her. For as many times as she said she was fine, I could tell she was shaken up. Of course, Malone hadn't helped.

He'd been pretty worked up when he found us there. But that was nothing compared to when it came out I'd been poking my nose where it didn't belong. His words, not mine.

Apparently he'd already cleared Jo as a suspect, and somehow it was now *my* fault she'd taken a face plant into a bus. When I told him about Cliff, he yelled at me in his I'm-going-to-throw-you-in-jail voice to stay out of it.

So I went home to Missy and to wait for Grey.

Mitch was running on the beach. (He'd finally talked to our mama. Enough said.) Nikki was packing.

"You don't have to leave." I sat crossed-legged on the bed and unpacked as she packed.

Nikki sighed. "Mel, you've been very gracious, but you have a lot going on here."

I got on my knees and dumped her suitcase contents all over the bed. I smiled, satisfied with my work. "You'll realize soon enough, if I have something to say, I'm just out there with it. If I wanted my place back or felt you two where cramping my style, I'd have put you up in the Montage."

Nikki tucked her hair behind her ears and stared wide-eyed at the pile of clothes. "You're exactly like your brother described."

"Feisty?" I jumped up and hugged her. "Come on, you guys don't have to leave tonight." I stepped back and grabbed her hands. "You haven't even met Grey. Stay. We'll take you guys to dinner at Mozambique. You'll love it. They have the best sweet potato fries."

She studied me, looking for something. I had no idea what. "You've just witnessed someone getting hit by a bus. On a scale of one to ten, how freaked out are you?"

I squeezed her hands, then let go. I plopped on the bed with a bounce. "A three. We just saw the aftermath. The actual face plant into the corner of the bus was missed."

Nikki blinked rapidly, then burst out laughing. "I thought Mitch was exaggerating about his family."

"Sugar, there's no stretching of the truth needed where the Langstons are concerned," I said in the thick Texas accent I'd worked to hard to lose.

A loud and obnoxious banging interrupted our giggle fest.

"Someone's really mad," Nikki said, looking toward the door.

Who was interrupting our bonding moment? Caro? Had she already discovered I had the brooch?

"Open the door," Cliff's drunk voice bellowed. "I know you're in there."

Definitely not my lovely cousin.

"I'll be right back." I made my way to the door and opened it a crack. "Didn't we just talk this morning?"

"Shay outta my life," he slurred.

Someone was drunker than a skunk. And smelled like one, too. "You killed your ex-wife."

"Nooo." He shook his head, slacked-jawed, as he spoke. He looked a little like Missy when she shook.

I don't know why I was arguing with a drunk man, but it seemed I was glutton for more Malone punishment. It wouldn't matter to him that Cliff had sought me out.

"Jo's dead," I said. I opened the door wider. "It had to be you. You showed up at her place and argued about money. When she told you she wasn't giving you any more money you got angry and whacked her with Fluffy's Emmy."

"You're a liar." He got right up in my face, his dragon breath singeing my eyebrows.

Nikki appeared behind me with my Louisville Slugger. My back up. "Do I need to call the police?" she asked, making sure Cliff could see the bat.

"Yes," I said.

"No," Cliff growled. He swayed back and forth as he stepped back.

I'm sure he was having visions of a different bat coming at him.

"Hey, I know you." Nikki pushed her way in front of me and poked Cliff in the chest with the bat. He almost landed on his rear, but managed to right himself. "What are you doing here? Are you following me?" she asked.

Cliff wiped the sweat off his forehead. "I don't know you."

"Yes, you do. I'm Nikki Espinoza. Well, now I'm Nikki Langston. I'm one of the pit bosses at the Luxor casino."

"Congratulations." He saluted her with his right hand.

"It's you." She turned to me. "I kicked him and his card counting brother out of my casino. They're lucky they're not banned from The Strip."

"When did you kick him out?" This was news to me. No wonder Cliff was so surly.

"A couple of weeks ago."

Cliff swayed back and forth trying to focus on Nikki. "You look different."

"Do you remember what day of the week that was?" I asked Nikki.

"Sure. It was a Monday. I only work Fridays through Mondays. Why?"

I swung around to face Cliff. That was the night Mona had died. "You've been telling the truth. If you were still in Vegas, there's no way you could have been here."

"I told you I didn't kill Mona," he yelled just before he passed out on my front step.

Chapter Thirty-Five

I left a voicemail for Malone, letting him know I had Cliff and Ted's alibi staying at my house. If I had to guess, he was still tied up at the accident scene aka crime scene. And we all knew how he felt about his crime scenes.

Come to find out, he'd left a number of messages for Nikki the last couple of weeks, but she'd been on her honeymoon in Thailand (no wonder Mitch wasn't returning Mama's calls). Nikki thought it would be better if she broke the news to Malone that she was my sister-in-law. Personally, I think she liked sharing quasi-bad news as much as I did.

I'd also left Grey a voicemail and a text to call me.

Drunk Cliff was momentarily awake and crying like a baby in my driveway. There was no way on God's green earth I'd let him in my house in his condition. It was a little cloudy out, not cold by any means, so sitting outside in short sleeves wasn't hurting him any.

Seriously, he was still wearing yesterday's clothes. Who knows what he'd been doing since I'd seen him at breakfast. I glanced at his Land Rover, the front tire hopped-up on the curb in front of my house. I take that back, it was obvious what he'd been doing. And now we were all paying the price.

It was supposed to rain later this evening, which could prove to be a good thing if Cliff tossed his cookies in my driveway.

Nikki and I hung outside with Cliff while we waited for Malone. She handed him a mug of coffee (I had no idea I even had coffee in my house; it must have arrived with my guests).

He accepted it grudgingly. "You think you're so smart. You don't know anything," he sniffled.

"You're not going anywhere. Fill us in." I was eager to hear what he had to say.

My neighbor, Endor, a white haired eighty-something, poked her head out her front door and yelled across the street in her shaky voice. "Do I need to call the cops?"

I waved her off. "They're on their way. Thanks."

She waved back and disappeared inside her house.

"Mona made some bad investments," he said.

"Like what?" Nikki asked.

"More like who. She invested in Cliff, and he gambled away her money," I said wryly.

"I know someone, who knows someone, who . . ." He rubbed his jaw, collecting his random thoughts.

Nikki looked at me wide-eyed. "This is going to take a while," she said under her breath. "I'm going to grab a couple of the beach chairs I saw in your garage."

"Great idea."

Cliff watched Nikki walk away. "I know someone who paints. I paid him to make me copies," he said.

"Forgeries."

"No, copies. Authentic museum quality copies." He sounded like an internet ad.

"What happened to the originals?"

"I sold them."

"Why didn't Mona turn you in?"

"She needed the money, too. She hated it." A satisfied smile settled on his lips.

"Did anyone else know about this?"

He nodded, then held his head one handed and groaned in pain. "Tricia and Jo knew she ran out of money."

"Are you sure?" That couldn't be right. Tricia had acted as shocked as the rest of us that Mona was broke. I stared at Cliff, who'd also acted surprised. Apparently they were all better actors than I'd given them credit for.

"They knew. That's why Jo was mad at Mona. She'd never paid. Not a single penny."

And now Jo was dead. Nikki reappeared with my favorite white and blue-striped chairs. They were still sand-encrusted from the last time I'd used them. She opened one and handed it to me.

"Thanks." We set up a couple of feet from where Cliff sat on the cold pavement. I don't think he even noticed.

"Were you and Jo having an affair?" I asked.

He hesitated. "We might have fooled around a time or two."

I wondered if that was why she ran. "What's the deal with Fluffy's pet recorder?" I still hadn't found the time to watch that silly thing.

"Hey, that's mine. Give it back. I bought that to spy on Mona." He tried to stagger to his feet, but failed miserably.

Nikki and I shared a look of disbelief.

So, it wasn't Mona's. Had Alex known, and that's why he'd brought it to me?

"Mona called it her insurance," I told him.

"Yeah, it recorded me and Jo messin' around. And there might be some footage of me carrying out a couple of paintings."

It really was her insurance. Mona was a smart cookie.

Not so smart as to keep from getting herself killed, but she'd been good at keeping tabs on those around her.

Cliff looked up at me, his face wan in the sun. He squinted his eyes. "I think I'm going to be sick." He weaved like a willow tree in a windstorm, then passed out cold.

"Is he always like this?" Nikki asked.

I shrugged. "Night night, cowboy. Pleasant dreams." He was going to have one doozy of a hangover in the morning.

Chapter Thirty-Six

Once Cliff had passed out, there was no more getting information out of him. Nikki helped me load him into my Jeep, and I drove him to Dana Point. He wasn't sleeping off his bender in my driveway. We'd figure out how to get his Land Rover to him later.

I called Grey before I left and filled him in on where I was headed and what Cliff said. Neither one of us completely believed Cliff. We agreed Grey should drive down to Dana Point and see the paintings first hand. He'd be at least thirty minutes.

I pulled into same parking lot as last time, only this time I parked as close to the dock as possible. I looked over at Cliff, slumped against the door. His drunken breath fogged the passenger-side window. Man, he stank.

Cliff's mouth dropped open, and he started snoring. There was no way I'd be able to get him to his yacht without help. Hopefully, Bruce would be on duty, and he could help me.

I was torn about leaving Cliff, but it wasn't as if anyone was in the market for a passed-out-drunk-fifty-something white man with zero money.

I locked the Jeep, then headed for the security office. I rounded the corner and ran into none other than Tricia Edwards.

"What are you doing here?" She looked around the dock and blushed.

Had I caught her in the act? Was this where her married man lived? "Cliff passed out drunk on my driveway. I brought him home."

She blinked. "Really? You have Cliff? You can't carry him all that way."

I shrugged. "I'm looking for Bruce."

"Who?"

"The security kid."

"Oh, I just came from the security office. No one's there. But I did see a wheelchair. I could grab that, and I'll meet you in the parking lot. Between the two of us we can get him to the boat."

"Great." I wasn't sure why she was suddenly being so nice, but I'd take it. Grey was on his way, but who knew how long he'd be. And in the meantime there was always the possibility that Cliff would upchuck in my Jeep.

I rushed to Cliff and positioned him the best I could so he'd fall into the chair. Tricia rolled up a short time later.

"I was thinking, if you hold the chair steady, I should be able to drop him in there like a bale of hay."

Tricia looked at me with unblinking eyes. She apparently didn't know what a bale of hay was. Since she didn't seem to have a better idea, I went with Plan A.

She positioned the wheelchair so it was parallel to the Jeep and set the brake. I grabbed Cliff by the waist and hugged him against me. I gagged when he exhaled.

"Oh my Lord, he reeks." I swallowed past the puke inching up my throat.

I took a deep breath and pulled him forward. He toppled out of the Jeep and onto me. I staggered under his weight. "Ugh." I quickly found my balance, then pivoted so his butt was aimed for the wheelchair.

"Here he comes," I murmured into his chest.

And there he fell.

I stared at his sorry drunken self. There was no way we'd ever get him on the boat. I'd have to wait for Grey.

"We have to get his keys," Tricia said.

I held them in front of me. "I grabbed them before you got here. He's really heavy. We're not going to get him on the yacht."

"We'll find a way. Even if we have to dump in the Pacific." Her eyes sparkled with a touch of vindictiveness.

Before I could say a word she was off with Cliff. I had half a mind to leave them both. As tempting as it sounded, I couldn't do that, not even to Tricia. I rushed to catch up to her.

I unlocked the security gate, and we strolled on through. It was easier getting onto Cliff's boat today than it had been with Darby.

"You didn't say why was Cliff at your house?" Tricia asked, looking straight ahead.

"He was going on about Mona and Jo. Did you hear about Jo?" I asked suddenly aware that she was really quiet and hadn't said a word about Jo's run in with public transportation.

She nodded. "Horrible." She picked up her pace.

Something Cliff said popped into my head. Both Jo and Tricia had known about Mona's finances.

My mouth suddenly went dry. I slowed down and started to assess my escape options. If Jo was dead, and Cliff had an alibi, and Darby really didn't do it, that left only one person.

Holy crapola.

She stopped in front of *Ruthless* and parked the wheelchair. "I see you've figured it out." Her voice was cold and lifeless. Just like Mona and Jo.

I took a step backward, but she grabbed my arm and shoved me against the yacht. It was totally unexpected.

She shoved something hard and cold into my side.

"Board," she ordered, ice dripping from her words.

Oh. My. God. Tricia killed Mona.

I was on autopilot. I was trying to remember everything I could about the yacht when Darby and I were here the other night. Was that just a day ago?

"What about Cliff?" I asked. "You can't just leave him in the wheelchair."

"Don't worry about that greedy idiot. I have plans for him, too. I'm framing him for your murder."

I swallowed. "I hate to break it to you, but I don't want to die."

She shoved me downstairs. I stood in the salon frantically looking for an escape.

"I don't understand, why did you kill Mona? You were friends." If Darby couldn't wrap her mind around a best friend sleeping with the husband, how was she ever going to accept murder?

Tricia paced, waving a wrench in front of her. That's what she's shoved in my back? I'd thought she had a gun. Dang.

"Mona wouldn't give me my money," she whined.

"She was broke. You heard Owen."

"She wasn't broke. Cliff was selling her art on the black market. If she was a real friend, she would have given me my money. We had a contract."

"The one you lost?"

"I didn't lose it. What kind of idiot do you take me for? She never gave me my signed copy. She hid it somewhere. That night, I demanded what was mine. I needed that money. She laughed at me. I was so angry, I hit her. I didn't mean to, but afterwards I was glad." Her lip curled with disgust.

"She laughed at everyone. Humanity was her private joke," I said. It was true. Tricia wasn't the only one Mona had belittled and demeaned.

"Well who's laughing now?" she asked, wild-eyed, slapping the wrench in the palm of her hand. "I wish I could say I'm sorry I have to do this, but I don't like you. Never have."

"I don't like you either. You should know, Grey's on his way."

She shot me a scorching look, cold and calculating. "Well, you've taken care of the last step for me. I was trying to figure out who would stumble upon you and Cliff. Now I don't have to worry about it."

Great. "Glad I could help with my own demise. Did you know about Darby?" I asked, stalling. Hurry up, Grey.

"I overheard Cliff and Mona arguing about her one night. And then after I'd killed Mona that little brat called. It was destiny. I just added three little letters, I-C-E, before her name, and it was perfect. Until you poked your nose in everything."

Wow, that phrase was really getting around.

Now, I have to admit the irony of the current situation wasn't lost on me. I'd sworn to Grey and Darby I would never allow myself to be held captive by a psycho hit man.

I'd never considered a wrench wielding psycho woman.

"You had to know I'd never let Darby go down for a crime she didn't commit."

Grey *had* to be here by now. I had no idea how he'd get past the security gate, but I had every confidence he'd find a way.

"It was fine when you were trying to prove it was Jo or Cliff. Then Jo was about to tell you about me and what I knew."

"What are you saying?"

"I pushed her. You know, the Laguna bus system is very timely."

She was mad. Crazy. A freakin' killer. Good grief, after two murders, what's one more?

"How?" My voice broke.

"She wasn't running from you. I saw her walking down the street and knew that was my chance to get rid of her, too."

A loud splash interrupted her tirade.

"Was that Cliff?" I asked.

She turned to look, and I shoved her into the mini bar and ran for the sleeping quarters. I shut the door and locked it. I pulled out my cell and called the cops.

Tricia started screaming obscenities—banging on the door with the wrench. I swallowed my fear. Lord, I hoped that door held.

In the background I could hear a loud booming voice shout,

"Police."

Thank God.

Tricia squealed and pleaded but from where I was hiding, the cops weren't having any of it.

Someone tried to open the door. "Melinda, are you in there?" It was Grey.

I unlocked the door and threw myself into his arms. "What in Sam Hill took you so long?"

Chapter Thirty-Seven

It had taken a good twenty-four hours, but our lives had settled down. Somewhat. All the way back to Laguna, Grey had lectured me on leading with my emotions and not my head. I knew he was talking more out of fear then anger, but that didn't lessen the sting.

Then we walked into my house, and there sat Detective Malone chatting it up with Nikki. I won't repeat exactly what he'd shouted, but it wasn't much different from Grey's lecture. I did worry briefly that Malone might just off me himself, he was so hot.

I didn't make any sweeping declarations, promising to stay out of his police work, but I did promise to keep my nose in my own business. I had to admit, if only to myself right now, once my life hadn't been in danger any longer, I seriously enjoyed the adrenaline rush of living on the edge.

Tricia was in lockdown at the Orange County slammer. Apparently I wasn't the only one she'd gone after with her wrench. Not only was she charged with two murders, but for assaulting a police officer and resisting arrest.

Rumor has it Cliff and his brother, Ted, left Dana Point. No one is certain if the brothers left on their own free will or if they got a one way ticket via the Pacific.

Fluffy was still camped out at Darby's. They actually like each other. Darby didn't know it yet, but I had an appointment with Owen Quinn on Friday. He agreed to file the paperwork to officially make Darby Fluffy's legal guardian.

Oh, and Alex had finally called and left me a voicemail. That stop in San Clemente was at a hotel. I'm guessing that's where Cliff and Jo had hooked-up. Mona must have taken Jo there to make her squirm just before she fired Jo O'Malley's phony animal communicator hiney.

Mitch and Nikki were leaving tomorrow. I guess Mitch wasn't much for crazy women welding a wrench. He'd tried to convince me Vegas was a quieter and safer place to live. I begged to differ. I loved my beachside community.

Grey was on his way over. The four of us were heading to Catalina Island for the day.

Nikki was in the spare bedroom packing. For some reason she'd asked my brother to keep me occupied.

I slipped on my jeans and a thick sweater for our trip, then cajoled Mitch to help me pack a picnic lunch.

"I hear Mama's throwing you small shindig." I slapped a healthy amount of peanut butter on a piece of whole wheat bread.

Mitch groaned and made a face I knew all too well, dread and doom.

"You know how she is," he complained.

"Oh, I'm well aware, 'Honey.' That's why I live in California. Mama's going to love Nikki. You picked a keeper." What I'd said was true, but it wouldn't stop Mama from asking Nikki to change her name to something more southern. I finished making the last PB&J sandwich and tossed the dirty knife in the sink.

Mitch pulled four plastic bottles of iced tea from the fridge and set them in the picnic basket. "You'll come to the party, right?"

"Absolutely." Once he was looking at me, I tossed him the sandwiches, and he dropped them in the basket, too. "I'm dragging Grey along as my deflector. Mama gets busy trying to impress my fiancé and forgets I'm there to nag. It makes for a more enjoyable visit."

Mitch pitched himself against the wall and studied me. "Speaking of visits. Nikki and I already agreed to go home for Christmas."

I didn't bother to look up from the mess on the counter. I knew where this was heading. "I'm sure you'll have an enjoyable time."

"Promise me you and Grey will come, too."

"I can't. Sometimes Grey has to leave unexpectedly." For an excuse it was pretty weak.

"You need to go home and see Mama and Daddy."

I sighed. "I will. For your party."

"It's not the same."

"I don't want to argue with you."

He crossed over to where I was standing and grabbed my hand. "Then agree to come for Christmas."

"Fine." Technically, I didn't commit to a specific Christmas.

Mitch's smile was so excited I had a twinge of guilt that I was already planning on a way to back out.

He snagged a cheese stick out of the basket and unwrapped it. "I had a nice chat with Caro yesterday. She looks good."

I swatted at him. "Stop eatin' the food. Caro's a Montgomery. It's genetically predisposed that she always looks good."

Mitch chuckled.

"What?" I asked, glaring at him.

"The two of you. You're exactly the same."

"Oh, no. I'm nothing like Caro. Where'd you see her?"

"She stopped by yesterday."

I dropped the peanut butter container on the floor and shrieked, "What?" I raced toward Fluffy's old room.

"What are you doing?" Mitch called out behind me.

I opened Fluffy's mini safe, which I had never locked. (I couldn't remember the combination. That's probably why Caro had made up one.)

A bounty of tiaras sparkled in front of me, but the brooch was gone.

Oh, she was bad. Bad, bad, bad. And I was stupid, stupid, stupid.

"Mitch," I whacked him on the shoulder, "I can't believe you just let her walk out of here with my brooch."

He looked at the safe and then at me. "Well, hell, Mel. How was I supposed to know that when she went to use the bathroom she was really sneaking around looking for that dumb pin?"

I just stared at him.

"Now it makes sense. But at the time . . ." He trailed off. "I'm sorry. Wow. She's kinda devious." He sounded impressed.

"You haven't seen devious. I'll get my brooch back. And I'll be wearing it at Christmas."

You'd better watch your back, Cousin. Here I come.

It all started...

With *Desperate Housedogs*

Excerpt

Chapter One

I don't normally break into people's homes, but today I was making an exception.

Not wanting to make the burglary too obvious, I'd parked my car down the street and fought through the bougainvillea hedge to the back of the house. In southern California the bougainvillea blooms everywhere, luxurious but tough, like old starlets wearing too much pink lipstick. Determination thumped in my chest but I was still as nervous as a long-tailed cat in a room full of rockin' chairs. Glancing left and then right to make sure none of the neighbors were around, I flipped up the sand-crusted mat and grabbed the key that lay under it.

My cousin, Melinda, always kept her spare key in the same spot. This particular mat said, "Wipe Your Paws."

Mel's place was nice. Not posh, but very nice even by Laguna Beach standards. Not at all like the open spaces we'd grown up with in Texas but nothing to sneeze at. Palm trees and Jacaranda trees surrounded her patio, and morning was already warming the ocean breeze. I unlocked the door and slipped inside. If I were lucky I'd find my target right away and get out quick. If I were really lucky, it would be a few days before Mel realized the brooch was gone.

I stepped into her sunshine-bright kitchen and noted the stack of dirty dishes. I truly wished the girl wouldn't leave dishes in the sink. Here in the semi-desert you run the risk of bugs. Bugs the size of cocker spaniels.

Eww. I shivered, shaking off the thought like a wet dog shaking off summer rain.

First, I checked the freezer. Not a very original hiding place and not a very effective one either, as I myself had discovered. I'd tried freezer paper and a label that said "Pig Hearts" but Mel had figured it out.

Okay, nothing in there.

Missy, Mel's bulldog, lumbered into the kitchen, her only greeting an eye roll that said, "Oh, it's just you."

I reached down and scratched behind her ears. She leaned into the ear rub. "If only you could talk, sugar. You'd tell me where Mel put it, wouldn't you?"

Missy gave a low, snuffly bark and butted my hand, effectively sliming it. Bulldogs are pretty darn loyal. Could be she wouldn't give up the hiding spot even if she knew. She waddled back to the living room and her spot by the picture window, as if to say, "You're on your own, girl."

"Fine, Missy. You're as stubborn as your mama." I wiped dog drool on my jeans and got back to the task at hand.

Hmmm . . . where would my beautiful (but devious) cousin put the thing? Like a bad Texas summer heat rash, irritation prickled.

Geez Louise, Mel, how long would it have taken to clean up after yourself?

I ran water in the sink and started stacking plates in the dishwasher.

See, that was the problem. Mel's not a bad kid, and only a couple of years younger than me, but she's so dang impulsive it seems I'm always cleaning up her messes. Take Mel's fight with the zoning board over not getting a permit for her new patio or her on-and-off again relationship with Grey Donovan.

Grey is a prince (in the metaphorical sense) and is caught in the unfortunate position of having befriended two headstrong southern women with a competitive streak. We'd inherited it—the competitive streak, I mean. Our mamas had both been Texas beauty queens, and we'd both lived the pageant life—for a while.

That's to say, until we rebelled. We'd each defied our mothers in our own unique way. Mine a little pushier, but straight-forward. Mel's a little wilder and out there. But then that kinda sums up everything y'all need to know about the two of us.

More about that later. Right now I had some searching to do before my cousin came home or her *lovely* neighbors called the cops.

I tried her bedroom, the study (junk room in Mel's case), the bathroom (I was happy to see she was still on her allergy meds), the closet (smaller junk room) and still came up empty-handed. Now, I was back to the kitchen.

Stumped, I stood and looked around, hands on my hips, arms akimbo, mind on hyper drive. It was a funky kitchen but decorated more for fun than utility. Mel's cookie jar was in the shape of a golden retriever. It was just flat adorable, the dog in a playful ready-to-pounce position. I wondered where she'd gotten it. If we were speaking, I'd ask her. But we're not.

I couldn't help it. I shook my finger at the cookie jar. *Melinda Langston, you should not be living on junk food and sweets.*

Her freezer'd been full of microwave dinners and her refrigerator completely devoid of any healthy fruits and vegetables. Probably living on processed food and sugar.

Still, Mel had always been a fabulous cook. She just didn't necessarily follow a recipe. The girl was a bang-up baker though, and cookies were her specialty. My mouth watered. One cookie would never be missed.

Don't mind if I do, cousin. I lifted the dog's butt to help myself and plunged my hand in the cookie jar.

Well, for cryin' in a bucket! Was the dang thing empty?

I couldn't believe I'd made the decision to indulge in empty calories only to be thwarted. I rooted around the inside of the cookie jar, my fingers only touching smooth pottery.

Wait. What was that?

Instead of cookies, my hand connected with metal. Grandma Tillie's brooch. She'd put Grandma Tillie's brooch—*my* brooch—in a cookie jar.

I pulled it out, brushed off the cookie crumbs, and turned it over carefully to check for damage.

Grandma "Tillie" Matilda Montgomery's brooch is the ugliest piece of jewelry you've ever laid eyes on. A twenty-two karat gold basket filled to the brim with fruit made from precious stones. Diamonds, topaz, emeralds, rubies. It is beyond garish.

Garish and gaudy, but significant. In her will, Grandma Tillie had left it to her "favorite granddaughter." I knew she meant to leave it to me. Mel was just as convinced she'd left it to her.

I prodded it with my finger. One of the emeralds might be a teeny bit loose. Promising myself I'd check more thoroughly for damage when I got home, I tucked the brooch in the outside pocket of my handbag and gave it a little pat.

Back with me, where it belonged.

I finished stacking the dishwasher, turned it on, called good-bye to Missy (who ignored me), and let myself out the back. I was just replacing the key when my cell phone rang.

"Hello." I answered in a low tone. No need to alert the neighbors. I'd made it so far without drawing any attention. Making my way to the front of the house, I walked quickly toward my car.

"Hey, Caro, this is Kevin. Kevin Blackstone." He sounded frantic. But then I'm used to frantic clients. "I need your help."

Oh, I don't think I mentioned it, but I'm Caro Lamont, and when I'm not breaking and entering, I'm the proprietor of Laguna Beach's Professional Animal Wellness Specialist Clinic. (The PAWS Clinic for short).

I'm not a dog trainer. Tons of other folks are more qualified in that arena. I basically deal with problem pets, which as a rule involves dealing more with the behavior of the humans than the pet. If I suspect a medical problem I refer pet parents to my veterinarian friend, Dr. Daniel Darling.

I could hear the deep barks of his two German Shepherd dogs in the background. It sounded like Kevin had a problem.

Kevin lived in the exclusive Ruby Point gated community just off of Pacific Coast Highway, (fondly referred to as PCH by the locals).

With all the noise, I couldn't hear what it was Kevin needed.

"I'll come by in a few minutes."

I think he said, "okay" but it was difficult to tell over the chaos on his end.

Extremely pleased with myself over the successful retrieval of my inheritance, I climbed in my silver vintage Mercedes convertible. Humming, I thought about the brooch, *my* brooch, safe in my handbag.

It was turning out to be a beautiful day in lovely Laguna Beach.

Life was good.

Acknowledgements

We'd like to acknowledge our critique group, Christine, Cindy, Laura and Tami, who unselfishly share their time and knowledge at the drop of a hat. We couldn't have done this without you.

To our rescue pets who provide us with inspiration and unconditional love, Sparkle, Abby, Chewy and Sophie.

Once again we are grateful to the wonderful people in Laguna Beach, CA. We apologize for the creative license we've taken with your amazing community.

To the talented team at Bell Bridge Books who continue to believe in Team Pets, you're amazing. Britt, your enthusiasm is boundless. Your emails make us smile. To the awesome editor, DebS, you made GF a better book. Thank you. DebD and DebS, we continue to be grateful for the guidance, knowledge and encouragement you share.

Last, but never least, to our husbands and our families. You touch our hearts daily. Without you . . . well, we'd get a lot more writing done, but our lives would be very boring and much less fulfilling.

The Pampered Pets Mysteries

Desperate Housedogs

Get Fluffy

Coming Next: Kitty Kitty Bang Bang

About Sparkle Abbey

Sparkle Abbey is the pseudonym of two mystery authors (Mary Lee Woods and Anita Carter). They are friends and neighbors as well as co-writers of the Pampered Pets Mystery Series. The Pen name was created by combining the names of their rescue pets – Sparkle (Mary Lee's cat) and Abbey (Anita's dog). They reside in central Iowa, but if they could write anywhere, you would find them on the beach with their laptops and depending on the time of day, with either an iced tea or a margarita.

Mary Lee

Mary Lee Salsbury Woods is the "Sparkle" half of Sparkle Abbey. She is past-president of Sisters in Crime – Iowa and a member of Mystery Writers of America, Romance Writers of America, Kiss of Death, the RWA Mystery Suspense chapter, Sisters in Crime, and the SinC internet group Guppies.

Prior to publishing the Pampered Pet Mystery series with Bell Bridge Books, Mary Lee won first place in the Daphne du Maurier contest, sponsored by the Kiss of Death chapter of RWA, and was a finalist in

Murder in the Grove's mystery contest, as well as Killer Nashville's Claymore Dagger contest.

Mary Lee is an avid reader and supporter of public libraries. She lives in Central Iowa with her husband, Tim, and Sparkle the rescue cat namesake of Sparkle Abbey. In her day job she is the non-techie in the IT Department. Any spare time she spends reading and enjoying her sons and daughter-in-laws, and four grandchildren.

Anita

Anita Carter is the "Abbey" half of Sparkle Abbey. She is president of Sisters in Crime – Iowa and a member of Mystery Writers of America, Romance Writers of America, Kiss of Death, the RWA Mystery Suspense chapter, and Sisters in Crime.

She grew up reading Trixie Belden, Nancy Drew and the Margo Mystery series by Jerry B Jenkins (years before his popular Left Behind Series.) Her family is grateful all the years of "fending for yourself" dinners of spaghetti and frozen pizza have finally paid off, even though they haven't exactly stopped.

In Anita's day job, she works for a staffing company. She also lives in Central Iowa with her husband and four children, son-in-law, grandchild and three rescue dogs, Abby, Chewy and Sophie.

CPSIA information can be obtained at www.ICGtesting.com
Printed in the USA
LVOW06s1825181114

414334LV00007B/826/P

9 781611 941210